Exuma Tide

A Bimini Twist Adventure

By

Patrick Mansell

Exuma Tide

A Bimini Twist Adventure

By

Patrick Mansell

For information contact:
Bimini Twist Adventures, Inc.
2911 N.W. 27th Ave.
Boca Raton, FL 33434
(561) 451-3452

ISBN 0-9676853-1-1

Graphics Design by Paul Hammond– Studio 41, Boca Raton, FL

Manufactured in the United States of America

Table of Contents

Dedication

Salt spray in our faces,
Warmed by the Sun
Trolling and dreaming of tournaments won
Life won't ever get better than this
Me and the boys on board Bimini Twist

From the Song "Bimini Twist"
Words and music by Lisa Mansell
Arranged by Charles Calello

ONE

Fearless Flyer

The same weather system that brought near record surf to the east coast of Florida was drenching the crews in the Bahamas Wahoo Championship. Ten foot swells with six foot chop had all but the sturdiest of sailors leaning over the rails. After three hours of trying to keep the big boats on a steady heading at seventeen knots, the captains, one after the other, set courses for North Bimini. The hours of buffeting around in a much too rough sea was taking a heavy toll on the fleet. While no hull damage had been reported, and there was no threat of capsizing, sinking, or loss of life, the salons, galleys, and sleeping quarters inside the boats were being badly tossed. The anglers and mates in the cockpits could hear the sounds of crashing kitchenware and sliding furniture coming from inside the cabins. It was time to slow the throttles and get out of this mess.

The weather was often bad in these winter tournaments, and the taking of wahoo, pound for pound one of the strongest and fiercest of the blue water prizes, was a challenge to any fisherman regardless of his skill level. Things could become very busy when the anglers had double headers to land. Gaffer Carson was on his first assignment as a mate for a major tournament. He was known as a capable boat handler and expert fisherman, and there was never any doubt that he was up to the task, but until now he had been too young to work as the sole mate in one of these dangerous cockpits. He was in complete agreement that it took a great deal of experience and maturity to do this job.

Gaffer was not disappointed when he heard the big diesels of *Fearless Flyer* slow their tempo to an idle. He stepped back to the transom to look up at the fly bridge. Captain Billy Bray looked down at the expectant anglers from his perch high on the bridge. He ran the side of his index finger across his throat. There was no mistaking his meaning. This day of fishing was over. Expecting to see disappointment in his guests, he was surprised to find more looks of relief than anything else. Like a good mate Gaffer made no comment. He merely sat on the starboard gunwale and began reeling in the wire line. When the thirty-two ounce lead cleared the surface of the water, he lifted it over the transom and placed it on the deck. He then hand lined the thirty foot, 500 pound test monofilament shock cord and wound it onto the deck. Next he lifted the heavily weighted, artificial lure into the boat and lay it on the deck next to the coil of shock cord. When he had repeated this procedure with the line on the port side, he placed his two pinky fingers into his mouth, curled his tongue, and let out a loud whistle. Captain Billy turned when he heard the sound. Gaffer shot him a thumbs up; Billy returned it and increased the throttles to 2,500 RPMs. As *Fearless Flyer* headed toward port, Gaffer busied himself in the cockpit securing the rods, reels, and tackle. The anglers made their way into the cabin to get out of the elements and try to collect their energy after such a grueling morning.

    Fearless Flyer idled into the Big Game Club dripping salt water and with its galley well-tossed. The crew and fishing party were glad to be back on land. They knew that the shortened day would hurt their chances of showing up well at the weigh-in, but it was a compromise they would have to accept. They were off the best tide for wahoo fishing, and to continue taking the pounding from the huge Atlantic swells would be a waste of fuel and energy. Sometimes that's how a day of tournament fishing went and you had to accept it. On the other hand, this decision set them up for better chances on subsequent days.

The weigh-in went much better than they had hoped. They had only caught two fish, but a daily catch of two was all that could count for points in this tournament anyway. It gave them an even chance with the rest of the contestants, and they knew that the big boy they had caught might well be the biggest catch of the day, qualifying them for a lesser prize, but nevertheless placing them in the daily rankings.

Their two entries had a combined weight of 112 pounds, a sixty-nine pounder and a thirty-three. Sixty-nine was a good size and rarely did anyone beat that mark. Six teams showed up and weighed in. Gaffer was beginning to feel quite good as the weights came nowhere close to his team's. Then Captain Mark Philips along with mate Sandy Roberts, the only female mate in the entire tournament, showed with their entries. They did not have to place the wahoos on the scales for Gaffer to know he had been out-fished. The first, and smallest of the two entries weighed fifty-eight pounds. The largest weighed seventy-four. *Fearless Flyer* had been beaten in the overall weight category and the biggest fish category. A small crowd gathered around the first place crew and began congratulating them. By the time the remaining eight contestants weighed-in, *Fearless Flyer* had slid into fourth place. Billy Bray, ever the .optimist, made the effort to cheer Gaffer who seemed a bit depressed

"Look at it this way, Gaff. We're ahead of thirteen boats and only twenty-points behind the leader. Look, man, this is only the first day. We can easily slip into the money and they can easily fall behind. One day is nothing. We have three more days here. Our job now is to keep it close and to keep our spirits up."

"It's OK," said Gaffer, "I'm good. I know we're in good shape."

"I thought you looked kind of depressed about it," said Billy.

"For a minute I got jealous of that seventy-eight pounder. I never saw a wahoo that big."

"Yeah," agreed Billy. "It was a nice fish." he paused for a few seconds and added, "Come on, Gaff. I'll help you clean these guys up."

Gaffer tossed the days prizes into the dockmaster's wheelbarrow and he and Captain Billy rolled them over to the cleaning tables. They hefted the biggest wahoo onto the table and proceeded to cut off its head and slit open its belly. Billy tossed the guts to the pelicans that were swimming around the cleaning station, and Gaffer cut off the tail and tossed that to them as well. "You can go join the party," said Gaffer. "I'll finish up here."

Billy thanked him and headed back to the scales while Gaffer repeated the cleaning procedure on the smaller fish before washing down the cleaning table and returning to the boat with his forty pounds of wahoo steaks. Captain Billy stayed around tournament central while the tournament officials posted the day's final results. There was a lot of tournament money at stake and it was Billy's responsibility to see to it that he received all the points he had earned.

After Gaffer stored the fish in the on-board freezer, he filled a five gallon bucket with fresh water and soap and began cleaning *Fearless*

Flyer from the top of the tower to the waterline. He worked without stopping for an hour and a half, and before he knew it he was rinsing and storing the cleaning gear and wiping down the windows. That job was finished and he had the rest of the day to himself.

The tournament contestants milled around the weigh-in station until after 6:00 PM. Gaffer rejoined them to check on the final results. It was official, with the last of the wahoo weighed and counted, *Fearless Flyer* ended the day fourth out of seventeen contestants. Not a bad result, but not in the money either. They would have to fish a lot harder and hope for some luck for the next three days to stay in the competition. But for a first prize of $100,000, and the Calcutta, a side bet that surrounded every fishing tournament, in the neighborhood of $65,000, for which *Fearless Flyer* had put up $5,000; fishing hard for four days was something to which the entire party had committed.

Billy Bray, Gaffer, and their three anglers joined the tournament party that was already in progress at the swimming pool of the Big Game Club. Induced by an abundance of the host's famous rum, several of the anglers, and a few of the crews, were beginning to be very loud and obviously quite drunk. This was not a scene with which Gaffer was comfortable, so he excused himself and left the Big Game compound and headed 200 yards to the south to the Compleat Angler. It was not the bar atmosphere that he cared about in the least. It was just that the Angler was a place to meet up with other buddies from around the island and talk about things. That could mean a discussion about the day's fishing, a game of ring toss, or just watch a basketball game on the TV. While the Angler could get quite loud and jumpy, Gaffer always enjoyed it. The walls of the bar were the unofficial historical register of

5

Bimini big game fishing. Decades of fishing history in the form of photos and drawings covered the walls. An entire room was dedicated to Hemingway's fishing exploits in Bimini, including early pencil sketches from The Old Man and the Sea. For people who loved fishing lore, the Compleat Angler was like coming home. Gaffer chose this spot to relax over the boisterous atmosphere surrounding the tournament. He walked up to the bar and ordered a coke. As he waited for his drink to be poured, his brother sat down along side of him.

"How'd it go?" asked P.J.

"What?" asked Gaffer.

"What else? The tournament."

"Oh, the tournament. Yeah." Gaffer continued, "We're in fourth place right now. It's really been ugly out there so we fished less than a half a day. Whoever wins this tournament is going to have to work for it." After a brief pause he asked, "Did you hear from Dad?"

"The flight canceled," said P.J. "He'll be here tomorrow."

"Why did the flight cancel?" asked Gaffer.

"They didn't say," replied P.J.

Gaffer appeared disappointed. "He was supposed to be fishing with us for the next three days. I could use his help in the cockpit."

"Well, you're on your own," said P.J. "He won't be coming."

Gaffer thought for a few seconds. "I'm going to call him." He rose from the bar stool and headed out the door with his coke in his hand. P.J. followed. Together they walked back up the road to the Big Game Club. As they passed the pool area they could hear the party still going strong, louder than ever. They entered the marina office and Gaffer asked the counter clerk for an outside line. It took several minutes to connect to mainland Florida, but finally he was talking to his father through a static-filled connection that sounded like it was bouncing off satellites in another galaxy.

"What happened?" asked Gaffer.

"There was a maintenance problem," said Max Carson. "There was nothing they could do. The earliest I can get there is tomorrow evening. Sorry, Son."

"I could sure use you in the cockpit," said Gaffer. "It was rough out there today. We fished three hours and gave it up."

"Catch anything?" asked his father.

"We only landed two wahoos, but they have some pretty good size."

"How did you make out in the standings?" asked Max.

"Fourth out of seventeen boats. I heard that two boats are quitting the tournament. Their crews and anglers were seasick the whole time. They just said the heck with it and decided to stay in."

"That rough, huh?"

"It doesn't bother me," said Gaffer. "I can work in the cockpit, it's protected. But Captain Billy is getting drenched on the flying bridge. It's open, and when we're high speed trolling the spray is fifty feet in the air."

Max's fatherly concern kicked in. "Son, you be careful back there. I don't want to hear about you falling overboard or anything. Are you sure you can keep safe?"

"Billy said if it's that rough tomorrow, everyone who wants to go in the cockpit will have to wear a life vest." After a brief hesitation he added, "Normally I'd grumble about that, but I can see he's right."

"Good," said Max. "You watch yourself tomorrow. Watch those wire lines and be careful with the fish you catch; those wahoos have been known to bite and they have strong jaws." After a brief hesitation he added, "And wear your deck shoes."

"Don't worry, Dad. No one is more cautious than me. We're being careful."

"How are your anglers?"

"Real good," said Gaffer. "They're all pretty experienced. They're real careful, and they know how to fish. It's a good party."

"I'm glad to hear that," said Max. "You don't need a bunch of amateurs back there when the weather is that rough."

"I agree," said Gaffer. "But don't worry, they're really good."

"OK, Son. You be safe and give my regards to Captain Billy. Tell him I'm sorry I couldn't be there tonight, but I'll see him tomorrow." Then Max added, "And please be safe. Do you hear me?"

"I hear you, Dad. Don't worry about me. I'll see you tomorrow."

When they hung up Gaffer felt much better. He knew that if the weather tomorrow were as bad as this day had been, they would come in early again. The tide change they were looking for would be at 10:20 AM, which meant they would not have to get up before the sun and cast off at the crack of dawn. They would have two hours in the morning to have breakfast, fuel the boat and prepare to cast off. The weather forecast was calling for a cool, sunny morning with stiff winds out of the northeast. It would probably be a day a lot like today. This was much to the disappointment of everyone on board *Fearless Flyer*. It was not the rough seas that bothered them so much as the prospects for a shortened day. Already behind the leaders in the tournament, they would have to fish long and hard to catch up. No one was denying that the prospects for winning a great deal of money was weighing heavily on their minds.

At daybreak the thirty knot north wind howled through the outriggers of the sports fishing fleet docked at the Big Game Club. It was loud enough to wake Gaffer. The moment he became conscious he lay still and listened. He did not have to sit up and look out the porthole of his cabin to know what was going on. The wind, the waves lapping against the hull a few inches from his head, and the gentle rocking motion of the boat in its berth told him that fishing conditions would be awful out in the unprotected offshore waters. He rose slowly and made his way into the crews' head to make himself ready to face the day. Captain Billy and P.J. were still asleep in their bunks. The rest of the party was sleeping ashore in motel rooms in the Big Game Club.

Gaffer made his way up the four stairs and into the galley. Now he looked out the window and saw what he had dreaded most. The whistling wind spread sheets of foam across the harbor, the channel, and flats opposite the marina. Flags and pennants stood straight out from their poles. It was going to be a sloppy day.

TWO

Wahoo

The instant *Fearless Flyer* cleared the southern tip of South Bimini and headed west, it was smacked broadside by the seas it would be battling all day. Two, three, four rolls side-to-side, and P.J. fell out of his bunk and onto the cabin floor. He awoke with a start and pain in his shoulder and knee. First he came awake and then he became conscious. A notoriously deep and sound sleeper, it took P.J. a long time to register what he was doing, where he was, and how he had gotten there. The realization that he was at sea on a rocking boat, instead of on land with a solid footing under him, became a disappointing reality. He raised himself to his hands and knees and steadied himself in that position before attempting to stand in the rocking passageway.

On deck Gaffer was wearing not only his yellow foul weather gear, but also a bright orange life jacket and, as his father had urged, his deck shoes. The anglers were in the warm, dry salon; Captain Billy was on the bridge. Gaffer sat in the fighting chair in the cockpit waiting for the word to start paying out the wahoo lures. The sea was manageable thus far, only four to six foot wave action, and coming from the port side. But they were still in the area protected by North and South Bimini. To the southwest Captain Billy could see the bigger waves looking like a herd of elephants in the distance. This was where they would have to fish. They could not stay in the lee of Bimini, it was simply an inferior location for wahoo fishing. They needed to cruise at least six miles further south to the entrance to Gun Cay Cut to place themselves where the best fish could be found.

Without giving it much more thought, Captain Billy turned toward the south and away from the lee of the island. Within five minutes *Fearless Flyer* was in unprotected sea and pounding through waves seven to ten feet high. Gaffer turned around when he heard the cabin door slide open. There he saw P.J. holding on for dear life, and trying to make his way out into the cockpit.

"Hey, you forgot to leave me ashore," called P.J. "You were supposed to wake me so I could get off the boat."

"P.J., I woke you three times," said Gaffer. "Each time you told me you were awake and were up. Finally I had too much to do to worry about getting you up, so here we are. Welcome to big game fishing."

"Oh, man, I can't believe it. I have to stay on this boat all day. I won't be able to stand it. I'm going to be seasick, I'm sure of it."

"That's OK," said Gaffer. "Just do it over the side. Lots of people do." There was no sympathy in his voice.

P.J. staggered over to the gunwale and looked around. Before he knew what had hit him he was covered in the salt water spray of an eight footer. "You're going to need your foul weather gear and a life jacket if you're going to be out here," said Gaffer. "Captain's orders."

"I don't suppose we could get Billy to take me back to solid land. I'll even take South Bimini and bum a ride to the Big Game Club. I can't stand the thought of being out here all day. I'll be dead by the time we head back."

"I can't help you," said Gaffer. "The tide is in forty minutes and

11

it's going to take nearly that long for us to get down to Gun Cay. You're stuck with us."

"What if I talk to Billy?" asked P.J.

"It won't make a difference. We're here to fish, there's a lot at stake. You're stuck for the day."

P.J. was not going to settle for that answer. "I'm going to ask Billy anyhow."

"Before you do," said Gaffer, "put on a life jacket. He has orders to everyone that life jackets have to be worn in the cockpit."

Again P.J. was frustrated. He reentered the salon and headed down the passageway toward the utility closet that held the foul weather gear and life jackets. He donned both and proceeded back out into the open cockpit, and from there up the ladder to the bridge.

"Hey, Billy, can I talk to you?" asked P.J.

Billy turned around to see P.J. half way up the ladder. He laughed, "Well, sleeping beauty. How nice of you to pay us a visit. What's on your mind?"

P.J. completed his climb and stood alongside Captain Billy on the rocking fly bridge. "I don't suppose we could discuss your dropping me off on solid land so I can go back to Bimini, could we?"

Billy looked behind the boat. They were already two miles outside of the Bimini Channel; past the point of no return. "Sorry, buddy. I'm afraid you're along for the duration. No turning back now."

"That's just great!" exclaimed P.J. "I get seasick real easy, you know."

"Yeah, I know. You should have gotten off when your brother called you. He couldn't get you up."

P.J. was deeply disappointed. "So how long am I stuck out here?" he asked.

Billy looked around, checking out the horizon and checking his watch. "Sorry to have to tell you this, but we haven't put the first line in the water yet. The answer is that we'll be here either until we catch two very large wahoos, or until lines out at four o'clock, or until we get beat to death by the sea."

"What do you think?" asked P.J.

"To be quite honest," answered Billy, "Our best hope is that we'll catch two monster wahoos early and then head in. Our second best chance is that we'll get beat to death and have to quit. The least likely is that we'll make it to four o'clock."

"So pray for wahoo," said P.J.

"Sure," said Billy. "Pray for wahoo."

The violent motion on the bridge was beginning to get to P.J. He headed down the ladder and stood in the cockpit with his brother. "Gaffer, fish like you never fished before. Billy says if you catch two big boys we can go in. Otherwise we have to stay here until the sea beats our brains in."

"Yeah," said Gaffer. "That's what we did yesterday. I'll do whatever I can to catch the wahoo. A lot's riding on it. Yesterday we were only out here three hours. This is worse than that."

"So there's hope," said P.J.

"Better than that," said Gaffer. "Yesterday the water was a half degree warmer and the current was a mile and a half faster. Today's conditions are a lot better." Gaffer took a minute the let a few thoughts come together. He backed up to the transom and let out a loud whistle.

13

Billy turned to see what he wanted. Gaffer called up, "Can I put the lines out?"

Billy looked at his Global Positioning Satellite to check his actual speed. Twenty knots and they were now only fifteen minutes off the best part of the tide. They were five miles from Gun Cay. He looked at his watch and considered. Right here off Picquet Rocks was also a decent wahoo spot. In fact, this entire corridor in the four hundred foot range was excellent wahoo territory. He throttled back to ten knots. "Tell the anglers that we're going fishing," he called down. Gaffer gave a thumbs up and opened the salon door. He called in and told the anglers what he was doing. P.J. leaned over the side and chummed his first of the day.

Gaffer was sympathetic. "Hey, Peej, sorry to have to tell you this, but we can only have four people in the cockpit. You either have to go inside or on the bridge. I think you'll be more comfortable if you'll lay down on the floor of the salon." Then after a brief pause he added, "But if you're going to barf, come out and do it over the side."

P.J. fought the pitching deck all the way into the galley. He poured himself a ginger ale. This often settled his stomach in situations like this. He drank the soft drink and then lay down on the floor of the salon. Within twenty minutes was asleep again.

Billy had his ear tuned to the VHS radio for any signs of action. He had a few friends in the tournament who switched back and forth between channel twenty-two and twenty-four to communicate. Although sixty-eight was the official channel of the tournament, nobody transmitted any important information over that frequency. It was more for communication with the tournament committee. The talk between the fishermen was much more private. They all had things they wanted to be heard by some boats but not others, so they set aside prearranged channels on which to talk. Mark Philips on board *Sea Eagle* was probably Billy's closest friend in the tournament, and they talked to each other about every half hour. Thus far there had been no known wahoo action. A few of the boats wanted to fish the waters around Ocean Cay which in this weather was another forty five minute run. A few of the others decided to head north toward Great Isaac which, under the circumstances, would be about an hour and a half run. It was a lot of driving in miserable conditions, but you never knew when one of these fisherman's intuitions would pay off. Billy's attitude was that he and all the other wahoo fishermen had caught as many wahoo in the Piquet Rocks to Cat Cay area as anywhere else. Why go any farther?

Forty minutes into the tide, at 11:00 AM *Fearless Flyer* got its first hit. As the wire line peeled off the starboard reel and the rod twitched violently, Gaffer whistled up to Captain Billy. As soon as Billy looked around to see what Gaffer wanted he knew they were hooked up. He pulled back on both throttles and brought the speed down to ten knots. The line stopped screaming but it was taught and the rod continued to shake. Quickly an angler went to the rod and began reeling. Gaffer sat on the opposite gunwale and reeled in the second line to keep them from becoming tangled. When the lead was to the boat he moved the rod to a more forward rod holder which would get the lead weight, leader and lure out of the way. He then opened the transom door and latched it. He went over to the angler to see how he was doing. At that moment the one hundred foot mark slid through the eyes of the rod and onto the reel.

"How's it going?" asked Gaffer.

The angler, Curt Sikes, of Amarillo, Texas, was beaming. Of the three man team of anglers, he was the one who did not catch a fish the day before, nor had he ever caught a wahoo. "Fine, Son. I'll have this baby in here any minute now."

"Another seventy-five feet," said Gaffer.

Curt continued to reel like crazy when all of a sudden the silvery sided fish broke the surface of the water and jumped high in the air. Disappointment showed on Gaffer's face. "Sorry about that, Sir. Maybe next time."

The angler looked at Gaffer "What's the problem?"

"Don't worry," said Gaffer. "You'll get another turn."

"What are you talking about?" asked Curt. A moment later the snap swivel reached the eye at the tip of the rod.

Gaffer lifted the heavy lead into the boat and hand lined the leader. He wrapped the wire line around his hand, a maneuver his father had told him a thousand times not to do. He then yanked the barracuda into the cockpit. He looked at Curt. "Sorry, it's not a wahoo."

"It looks like a wahoo," said the angler.

"Kind of," replied Gaffer. He lifted the barracuda by its gill and worked to free the hook from its mouth, being very careful not to get a finger anywhere near the fish's sharp teeth. With a few twists and jerks the hook was freed from the nasty mouth. Gaffer held the cuda over the side and let it go. It had not been hurt, there was no blood anywhere, and when Gaffer let it go, it darted away. Gaffer shrugged at Curt. "Junk fish," was all he said. Curt was disappointed but he seemed to understand.

Within two minutes the lines were back in the water and *Fearless Flyer* was clipping along at a high speed troll. The seas were rougher now, and it was very difficult to move around the cockpit without holding onto something stationary to keep steady. On the bridge Billy was getting drenched each time the bow of the boat pounded through a new wave. The men in the cockpit were being soaked by the salt water spray flying up from the wake and the waves in the swirling wind. Curt's brother, Jessie, had lost the color in his face and promised to be the next one to get seasick. Gaffer explained how it was done over the side, and in no more than another two minutes Jessie was doing it too.

They were on the best tide of the day and Gaffer and Billy knew it. They both looked at their watches at the same time. They were now an hour into the tide and the bite would soon begin to fall off. It was near panic time for Billy. As he lifted his VHS to call *Sea Eagle* he heard Gaffer's whistle. Looking down, what he saw was huge waves, a treacherous wake, salt spray, and Gaffer running to the side of the boat. On the opposite side was a rod, bent over at a dangerous angle with the wire line screaming out. Curt Sikes sat on the gunwale as it came up and down under him, much like the mechanical bulls he sometimes rode in his neighborhood tavern in Amarillo. Gaffer silently respected the man for his toughness. What he was doing was not easy on the violently rocking deck.

The boat slowed and Curt reeled. Gaffer brought in the second line and stored the rod out of the way. He opened the transom door again, latched it, and walked over to where the angler was reeling. Curt was sweating this one. In fact, the fish gave so much resistance that Curt was reeling the two speed Duel 9/0 reel in reverse which was the low speed gear, reserved for the most strenuous of fights. Even in low gear he was straining to gain on the strong game fish. Gaffer looked up for a moment at Billy and saw that he had a horrified look on his face.

"What?" called Gaffer.

"I'm coming down," said Billy. His view from the bridge was much better than what the men in the cockpit could see.

"What?" repeated Gaffer.

"Huge," was all Billy said.

"Stay there, drive the boat," insisted Gaffer. "I'll handle this."

Billy returned to the helm. The snap swivel was now up to the tip of the rod. Curt's work was finished, Gaffer's was just beginning. "You'll have to bring the rod over to the fighting chair," Gaffer said to Curt. "Balance yourself as much as possible against the chair and then sit down. Hold on to that rod for all you're worth." Curt did as instructed.

Gaffer made his way to the transom door, holding the shock cord in his gloved hand. This was scary. The back of the boat was rising and falling, crashing with each new wave, and bringing ankle deep water into the cockpit with every bounce. Gaffer did not want to stand in the doorway as the smallest slip would send him overboard. It was the main fear on his mind as he used all his strength to haul the wahoo first onto the swim platform and then line it up with the door opening. As the stern of the boat rose from the water, Gaffer saw that the fish was nearly the full length of the beam. Couldn't be, the beam was over thirteen feet. His imagination was playing games with him. He had only one chance at this and he had to do it right the first time. The stern crashed back down into the water and the fish floated up with the motion, wildly bucking the whole time. As the wahoo became weightless in the water,

Gaffer moved it further toward the starboard side of the boat. The stern rose with the next wave and Gaffer gave a mighty heave on the line. The wahoo's head entered the boat. The fish was half in and half out of the transom when the next wave lifted the fish up and Gaffer floated it into the cockpit. He jumped aside as the fish passed by. He then moved behind the fish and closed the transom door. The fish was caught, it was in the cockpit bucking and fighting wildly. Curt raised his feet so as not to be a target for those nasty teeth. Gaffer moved to the opposite side of the cockpit, breathing hard and with his heart racing. How he was going to get this monster into the fishbox he did not know. But what he did know was that the fish was in the boat and was not going anywhere.

Captain Billy placed the throttles into neutral and quickly descended the ladder. The wahoo was beating itself nearly to death banging around on the deck. Billy shook his head and grinned. He looked at Curt and Gaffer. "A hundred pounds easy," he said.

Curt grinned. This would be the biggest fish of the day, worth $700 in the Calcutta, maybe the biggest fish in the tournament, worth ten times that amount. P.J. and Jessie came out to see the prize. While they were both adequately impressed, their stomachs overcame them and for the second time this day they headed for the rails.

When the fish had stopped its furious bucking, Gaffer took the leader line, Curt took the tail and Billy grabbed the fish around the middle. Together they hefted it into the fish box. Billy took a good look. The box was just barely long enough for this prize. It seemed to Gaffer and Billy that this kind of sloppy weather always produced the best fish, the only problem being how hard you had to work to accomplish that.

19

Two hours after landing the prize wahoo, *Fearless Flyer* backed into its berth at the Big Game Club. Before the first line was cast ashore to tie off, P.J., weak and disoriented, jumped across to the dock. Within minutes he was feeling better on account of the firm ground beneath his feet. He walked down the dock and climbed the stairs to the second floor bar where he ordered a bowl of conch chowder, a cheeseburger, and a coke. From his vantage point above all the action in the marina, he could see Gaffer and Billy secure the boat and begin the ritual of weighing in and washing down.

Luck had been with the *Fearless Flyer* crew this day. They caught a second wahoo before returning for the weigh in. This one was nothing like the first one, but it was respectable nonetheless. A crowd gathered around the wheelbarrow as Gaffer pushed it down the dock. The prize wahoo's head was sticking far out over the front of the cart while the tail stuck far out the back. By the time Gaffer and Billy reached the scales they were surrounded by every crew in the tournament.

Now was the moment of truth. It took Billy and Gaffer, with the help of one of the officials, to lift the huge fish onto the scale. Gaffer was holding his breath as the scales bounced back and forth before giving the final official readout. The fish was nowhere close to a world record, but it was by far the biggest wahoo caught this year in the Bahamas Islands. The final weight for the record was 112 pounds. Ooh's and ah's came from the crowd as Gaffer beamed and Captain Billy shook a dozen hands. Curt Sikes stepped into the middle of the crowd and posed with Gaffer and Billy as the winning angler and team. The thought crossed Gaffer's mind that this could be a picture worthy of a place on the wall of the Compleat Angler.

Fearless Flyer's second wahoo weighed in at thirty-six pounds. The party's total for the day was 148 pounds, easily the winner for the day and enough weight to put the team in overall first place for the tournament. Thrilled to be at the top of the leader board, Curt Sikes insisted on taking Gaffer and Billy upstairs to join P.J., were he treated everyone to a hearty late lunch. The atmosphere around the table was highly spirited as only a first place team can understand. It was an hour and a half luncheon with a lot of boasting and high praise for the crew who found and helped land that giant fish.

When the lunch was finished and the festivities died down, Gaffer and Billy returned to reality. They had 148 pounds of wahoo to clean and a boat that was filthy from stem to stern and needed a good bath. It was still early afternoon and Gaffer knew that if he worked fast he would be finished with his chores in time to meet the 4:20 seaplane carrying his father. He prevailed upon P.J. to help by starting to clean the boat while he dressed the fish. Billy, Gaffer, and P.J. worked as a team to complete their chores as quickly as possible.

At 4:00, when *Fearless Flyer* and the wahoos were all clean, and Gaffer and P.J. had both taken warm showers, they headed down Kings Highway toward the seaplane ramp to meet their father's plane. Gaffer could hardly wait to tell him about the tournament standings.

THREE

P.J. and Ashley

The flight from Fort Lauderdale on the seventeen seat Grumman Mallard Floatplane was flawless. It took off on time and landed on time, an occurrence that happened rarely. Max Carson stepped off the **plane** in Bimini and was happy to see his two sons waiting for him **at the** immigration building. The boys were smiling wide when their father appeared. They passed a few words back and forth before Max had to turn into the Customs Building to clear through. Five minutes **later** he emerged with his passport stamped and legal to travel freely ab**out the** Bahamas. Gaffer grabbed Max's small duffel while P.J. took his camera bag. Max was free to walk down to the Big Game Club unencumbered.

Gaffer could not hold back his excitement. "We're leading the tournament," he said.

Max was startled and delighted. "First place?"

"First place," said Gaffer effusively. "You should have seen this wahoo we bagged today. One hundred and twelve pounds; the biggest caught in the Bahamas this year."

Max was incredulous. "A hundred and twelve pounds! I've never seen one that big."

"Me neither," said Gaffer. "In fact, the dockmaster at the marina said he's never seen one that big, and he's seen about a million of them."

"A hundred and twelve pounds," repeated Max shaking his head and grinning. "Amazing." Then he turned to P.J.. "How ya doin', son? Having fun yet?"

"I'm good," said P.J. "I was with them when they caught it."

"You fished with them today?" asked Max. "I'm surprised. I thought you said you were staying ashore during the fishing."

"I didn't fish," said P.J. "I overslept and found myself a couple of miles offshore with no way back, so I was stuck for the day."

"And he didn't fish," said Gaffer. After a pause he added, "He did, however, chum."

Max made a face. "Fun, huh, P.J.?"

"Never again," came the reply.

When Max and his sons entered the Big Game complex the tournament party had already begun. Billy Bray had been handed so many rum punch cocktails that his eyes were watering, and his step was very uncertain. When he greeted Max it was immediately obvious that his speech was slurred and he was well on his way. Many of the sea captains drank way too much, and Max knew it. Billy had reason to celebrate, having landed the biggest wahoo of the year in the Bahamas Islands. For this he would be recognized in fishing journals and articles would be written about it. Max's only concern was that Billy would have a force five hangover tomorrow, which he would have to sleep off, leaving Max to man the bridge. He hated the prospect of joining the tournament from the bridge, a wet and violently rocking place that kept his stomach on edge the whole time.

"A drink for my friend here," slurred Billy, way too loud.

Before Max could protest somebody placed a Bahama Mama rum cocktail into his hand. He thanked the somebody and thanked Billy. So as not to insult his host, Max took a sip of the concoction before placing it on the wall of a concrete bougainvillea planter, to be picked up later by housekeeping.

"Billy, I'm going to go settle on the boat," said Max. "Where should I bunk?"

"You get the spare bunk in my cabin," said Billy. "The party is staying ashore, so we have the whole place to ourselves."

"I like that," said Max. "Care to show me?" Max was trying to urge Billy away from the bar, but it wasn't working.

"Naw," said Billy. "Gaffer can show you the way. I'm going to stay here and celebrate."

"Well, be careful," said Max. "You'll have to be alert tomorrow if you're to keep the first place position."

"I'm fine, I'm fine," said Billy. "I'm fine." He turned to walk away and nearly fell into the swimming pool before P.J. grabbed him and led him to a nearby chaise lounge. Billy sat down hard and soon passed out.

Gaffer showed him around the boat, where his bunk was, and how the head worked. After unpacking and changing into more comfortable island attire, a tee shirt, bathing suit, sandals and a wind breaker, Max climbed the ladder to the bridge. Gaffer followed right behind him. "What do I need to know about this boat for tomorrow?" asked Max. "I don't think Billy will be in any condition to help out."

"The only thing is that there is no communication between the cockpit and the bridge. If I want to get Billy's attention I have to whistle, and vice versa. It's been a rough sea and we can't hear each other well, and most of the time Billy is concentrating pretty hard on driving."

Max looked around the bridge at the instruments. He knew the GPS Chart Plotter, the depth finder, and the radar. The VHS was standard. The radar was not what he was used to so he spent a minute studying it. "What radio frequencies are we using?" he asked.

"Sixty-eight's the tournament channel. We go between twenty-two and twenty-four with *Sea Eagle*. Other than that, we keep pretty quiet."

Max looked around some more. Standard throttles, gear shift, trim tabs. Water temp, engine temp, battery AMP's, fuel sensor, starter switch, all familiar. In the salon Max found the electrical panel and opened the doors. Again there was nothing he had not seen before. "Two minutes in the engine room and I'll be done," he said to Gaffer, who in turn lifted the stairs leading down to the galley to expose the engine room. Max crawled in and looked around. He found the water intake, exhaust lines, and bilge output. He crawled back out and wiped his hands on a paper towel. "Life jackets?" he asked.

Gaffer showed his father where the life jackets and foul weather gear were stored. Feeling that his overall safety inspection was complete, Max took a seat in the salon to hang out with his boys. An hour of quality time with P.J. and Gaffer was just what the doctor ordered.

At 9:00 AM when the big diesels aboard *Fearless Flyer* came to life, P.J. was startled awake. He jumped out of bed and hurried into the head. As he took care of his business, he looked out the porthole to see that they were still tied to the dock. He emerged from the head and walked by the captain's cabin where he saw a huge pile of blankets and Billy Bray unmoving, in spite of the engine noise. He continued along the passageway, up the stairs to the salon and out onto the deck. Gaffer was in the cockpit with the anglers. Max was on the bridge. Excellent, there was still time to get off the boat before it pulled out. P.J. climbed half way up the ladder and called to his father.

"Dad, are you getting ready to take off?"

"Pretty soon, P.J. Are you going with us?"

"Not today. Yesterday was about all I could handle."

"It'll be better today," said Max. "The wind has died down some. It won't be that rough at all."

"Thanks anyway, but I'll just go get breakfast at Captain Bob's and then find a place to curl up and go to sleep."

"Suit yourself," answered Max.

As P.J. backed down the ladder and stood on the deck, Curt Sikes handed him his room key. "Here you go, son. In case you need a place to get out of the elements. It has TV and a comfortable bed.

P.J. was all set. "Thanks, Curt. I appreciate that. Good luck fishing today." P.J. then jumped across to the dock and helped Gaffer untie the dock lines. In another minute *Fearless Flyer* was idling out of its slip and headed over to the fuel dock 150 yards away. P.J. walked over to meet the boat again. He took the dock lines from Gaffer and wrapped them around the bollards to secure *Fearless Flyer* for its fuel-up. He was standing on the concrete dock which was a few feet higher than the gunwales of the boat. His father could look straight across at him.

"You sure you don't want to go?" asked Max.

"I'm sure," said P.J. "Mr. Sikes gave me the key to his room, so I'm going to go down to Captain Bob's and then maybe back to bed."

"You ought to take Captain Billy with you."

"Yeah, I saw him down there," said P.J. "Are you sure he's alive?"

"He's alive, barely," joked Max. "He's going to have a major hangover when he wakes. For the time being it's best to let him sleep as much as possible."

"If he wants to go with me he better come now," said P.J.

"I was only kidding," said Max. "When he wakes up he's probably going to want to do what he can to be the captain. The binge last night was just a one time indiscretion on account of all his excitement over the big wahoo, complicated by all his friends trying to help him celebrate."

P.J. stayed around long enough for Gaffer to finish filling the fuel tanks. He replaced the nozzle and ran the boat's credit card up to the marina office. Ten minutes later he was untying the dock lines and pushing *Fearless Flyer* away from the pier. He waved goodbye to the crew and headed out toward Kings Highway as the boat idled south to defend its first place position in the tournament.

The day was beautiful. Seas of three feet or less, water temp of seventy-two degrees, one knot current to the north. The sun was warm and the breeze was refreshing. It was a mild winter day, the best kind the tournament participants and officials could hope for. The VHS airwaves were abuzz all morning. Everybody from Great Isaac to Orange Cay was catching wahoos. By the time the tide had passed, *Sea Eagle* had already boated eight wahoos, four of which they were fortunate enough to be able to release, as they were smaller than some of the others that were already in the fish box. Similar stories were being told by the other contestants. And *Fearless Flyer* was getting its share. Gaffer released two of five hook-ups. He was certain that the two biggest fish were at least forty pounds each.

After the boat left, P.J.'s thoughts had returned to sleeping. He felt that since his brain was still half asleep, it would take no time at all for him to fall the rest of the way. He found Curt Sikes' room, a private bungalow only a few steps from the dock area. Not wanting to abuse his host's hospitality, instead of climbing into the bed, P.J. grabbed a comforter that had been knocked to the floor, and covered himself up on the living room couch. He was fast asleep in an instant.

The banging and clanging of the housekeeper was what finally caused P.J. to wake up. He looked at his watch and saw that it was already 11:00 AM. As the housekeeper began to quietly back out of the room P.J. called to her, "You don't have to leave. I'm up. Go ahead and straighten up the room. It'll just take me a minute to get my shoes on."

"I'll come back," answered the maid.

"Suit yourself," said P.J., "but I'll be out of here in no time."

"I'll come back," she repeated.

P.J. was soon on his way to Captain Bob's. He hoped that he was not too late as he knew they were only open for breakfast. To his delight, when he arrived at the front door to the restaurant, they were not only open, but there was a good crowd and they were likely to stay open for a while longer. He entered the restaurant and walked into the kitchen. There stood one of his favorite Bimini natives. When Gladys saw him she beamed and came up to him for a big hug, which P.J. was glad to give. They were old friends and were happy to see each other.

With the pleasant greetings done, P.J. returned to the dining area and took up a seat near the window. He reached into his backpack for a book he had been reading for an English assignment at the University. He set the book down and walked over to the breakfront against the wall where he poured a cup of coffee, and then returned to his seat. He gave his order to the waitress and sipped coffee and began to read his book. His mind went to thoughts about getting school work done in a relaxed, unhurried way.

P.J. could hear arguing coming from a table only a few feet away. It was a whispered argument, but he could still make out what they were saying. It seems that the girl had been promised a restful weekend in Bimini, and was looking forward to just that. The boy, on the other hand, had other ideas and his plans included romantic notions which were not to the young girl's liking. P.J. looked over at them and could see that the boy was red in the face, and his anger was about to explode. The girl's eyes were welled up and she was near tears. She had a most unhappy look on her face. P.J. looked away so as not to be conspicuous, but he listened just the same. The boy was being a complete moron while the girl, in the nicest way she knew how, being careful not to say anything any more offensive than necessary, tried to reason with him that she was not that kind of girl, and he had the wrong idea. P.J.'s own temper flared when he heard the boy call the girl a mean and ugly name, using expletives better reserved for a locker room or truck stop. The girl tried to hide her face, but it was more than obvious that her feelings had been badly hurt and she was crying.

P.J. rose from his chair and walked the few steps to the other table. He had a choice to sit next to the boy or the girl, as each had empty seats next to them. He sat next to the boy. "Hi," he said, "I'm P.J."

The boy looked startled and a bit annoyed. The girl looked embarrassed and tried to wipe her tears. P.J. handed her another napkin which she used to blow her nose.

"What do you want, P.J.?" asked the boy.

P.J. smiled at the girl, who seemed to be about his age. She was small and frail but even through her frown and tears, P.J. could see that she was very pretty. Her eyes, when not flooded with tears, were large and blue. Her blond hair was shiny and flowed to well below her shoulders. Her skin was browned by the sun, and very healthy looking. He understood why a guy would want to be alone on a romantic island with her. But Bimini was not a romantic island; it was more like a fishing village. Perhaps for this clod sitting next to him, a cheap place to get away with a girl like this, and make her life miserable if she did not give in to his advances. Coward was the first image that came to P.J.'s mind when he thought about the situation in which this boy had placed the girl. It made him mad.

With these thoughts in mind P.J. answered the boy's question. With a cold stare he said, "She's not interested in what you're selling. Why don't you give her a break?"

"Why don't you mind your own business?" said the boy.

The girl extended her hand to shake P.J.'s. He took it and held it for a little longer than necessary. She smiled at him for the first time and said, "P.J., it's very nice to meet you. My name is Ashley."

P.J. gave her his most beguiling smile and repeated, "Ashley." He released her hand and turned his attention back to the boy. He scowled

30

at him. "Did I hear you say you were leaving? There's something going on here and I don't think I like it."

"I didn't say that," said the boy angrily. "You're the one who's leaving."

"I don't think so," said P.J. Ashley was now composed. The dark mood was lifting. P.J. looked at her for a long moment. She really was quite beautiful. He turned back to the boy. "Now, what are we going to do?"

"I said, you're leaving," said the boy.

"What's your name?" asked P.J.

"What's it to you?"

P.J. placed his arm across the back of the chair in which the boy was sitting. It caused the boy to flinch. With his other hand he held the finger tips of the beautiful Ashley. She did not mind at all. So there he was, completely open, one hand on the back of the boy's chair, the other reaching across the table to touch Ashley's hand. "I want to know the name of the coward who is making this little girl cry." P.J. paused for a moment. He looked at Ashley and smiled. She smiled back. P.J. looked back angrily at the boy. He scowled, and through clenched teeth he growled, "What's your name, punk?"

The boy shrunk from P.J.'s hard look. Just as he was about to answer, the waitress came with the check for the table. P.J. snatched it from her hand and gave it to the boy. "Pay this and get out of here." The boy rose from his chair, fumbled through his pockets for some money and thrust it toward the waitress. Red faced, angry, and embarrassed, the boy stormed out of the restaurant.

P.J. released Ashley's hand and sat back. "I'm sorry about that,"

31

he said. "I hate conflict. I'm really a very peaceful guy. It's much too nice of a day to be quarreling."

Ashley composed herself. She sat back and said, "Thank you, P.J. That was very awkward for me. Bradley was not going to take no for an answer, and I'm stuck here on this island like a prisoner."

"Bradley," said P.J. with surprise. "Kind of a macho, manly name for a wimp."

Ashley laughed. At that moment the waitress returned with P.J.'s order. He pointed at her to place it where he sat. He decided he would join Ashley at her table while he ate. He dug into his food as if he had not eaten in days. Ashley was surprised at this. "P.J., how can you eat like that? Isn't your stomach upset from the confrontation with Bradley? Mine is all jumbled up, I couldn't think about eating."

"Why is your stomach upset?" asked P.J.

"You know, the confrontation."

"Oh, that," said P.J. "That wasn't a confrontation." After a pause he added, "Well, I mean maybe it was a confrontation for you, but it wasn't for me."

"But you're the one who stepped in. There might have been fight. You could have been hurt."

P.J. wiped toast crumbs from his mouth and sat back. He took a sip of his coffee, and took his time answering. "A couple of things you need to know. First, Bradley is a bully. Who would do what he did to you?"

"What do you mean?" asked Ashley.

"He was bullying you. Humiliating you and trying to scare you. Look, he's probably two hundred pounds. You're half that. He's a foot taller than you and must look like a giant to you, physically I mean. The fact is, there is nothing you can do if he wants to overtake you. He's not listening to your words; he's intimidating you with his size."

"You're right about that," said Ashley. "There's nothing I could do."

"So what kind of guy does that? Think about it."

"A bully."

"Exactly," said P.J. "A bully. And what kind of person bully's a girl half his size?" asked P.J.

"You tell me," said Ashley.

"Only a coward. Loud mouth, intimidating, overbearing coward."

"I guess you're right," said Ashley.

"So, you see," said P.J. taking another bite of his toast, "I was never in any danger. He's just a bully and a coward. I'm almost as big as him, so he would never try anything with me. I knew that all along, so I experienced no fear or anxiety." P.J. chewed and tried to smile. Then he swallowed he added, "Therefore I can eat, because my stomach is not upset."

For the first time Ashley laughed. Her face was bright and her eyes twinkled. She looked with admiration at P.J. "You know, P.J., you just never know where you might meet an interesting person. Here we are in Bimini, wherever that is, and we met each other."

"Are you saying you think I'm an interesting person?" asked P.J. Ashley could feel the blood rush to her face. P.J. could see the blush. "I'm sorry. I didn't mean to embarrass you. I'm a very straight forward person, but sometimes I ask embarrassing questions. I didn't mean to do that."

Ashley laughed again. She looked directly into P.J.'s eyes and answered coyly, "Well, you're something. You've already shown me that you're smart and brave. And, if I might say," she paused and the blush returned to her face as she considered for a moment. She was going to say she liked the way P.J. looked, but she decided to make it easy on herself, "you seem nice."

P.J. smiled, "Thanks for saying so. You seem nice too." After a pause in the conversation he spoke again, "I guess whatever your plans were with your friend have been canceled. Want to chill with me? I know the island pretty well."

"You mean there is actually something to do on this island?"

P.J. looked at her in puzzlement. "Heck no," he said. "If you've been here a day, you've probably done everything the island has to offer, unless you fish."

"No, I could never get into fishing," said Ashley. "I've done it a few times, and it always seems to end in blood and stink. Do you fish?"

"My fishing adventures always seem to end up in seasickness," said P.J. "I try to avoid it."

"Then why did you come to Bimini?"

"I'm here with my father and brother. They fish a lot so I come for a vacation. Sometimes when they go out, I'll go to the beach or a pool. Sometimes I study. Whatever."

"Oh, you're with your family. That's cool." After a hesitation she added, "I could use my family right about now. I don't know what I'm going to do about the situation with Bradley. I don't have my own room, and I don't even know about getting home."

P.J. felt sorry for her. It was like being shipwrecked on a remote island with no way home. Certainly she must by now feel stranded and a bit scared. "Where are you staying?" he asked.

"Right here, Sea Crest."

P.J. brightened. "OK, no problem," he said. "I usually stay at Sea Crest when I'm here. I know all the people who work there, so we know your belongings are safe. I'm sure when we tell your story to the manager she'll let you into your room to get them if Bradley won't. So there's no problem." He looked at his watch. "It's noon now. How about we forget about it for the next three hours. We can go to the beach if you'd like or to the pool at the Big Game Club or Blue Water. Then we'll do whatever seems like the right thing. We're going to have three hours of uninterrupted vacation with no worries about anything, Bradley, your accommodations, nothing. Just relax and see what comes up."

Ashley appeared concerned. "Usually when I have a problem like this I like to attack it right away. I don't like to leave problems hanging."

P.J. looked directly at her. "OK, then. What are you going to do?"

"I don't know," she said.

"Exactly," said P.J. "No solution in sight and you want to solve the problem right away. That's why I said wait three hours and by then you might have several excellent solutions."

Ashley laughed. "You might just be right," she said. "But I have to move out of that room. My stuff is up there and I want it out."

"Let's go," said P.J. He stood and led Ashley out. She gladly followed him. They walked around the back of Captain Bob's and up to the Sea Crest office which was only a few steps away. Fortunately the manager was in. P.J. stepped into the office and told the manager about Ashley's problem. She was sympathetic and accompanied Ashley and P.J. to the room. Bradley was nowhere in sight, so Ashley went in with the manager and quickly packed her clothes and toiletries into her suitcase. She located her plane ticket home and placed it in her beach bag. She scribbled a curt note to Bradley telling him that she would be leaving, and she would find her own way home. As she walked out of the room she felt a great sense of relief. The hotel manager graciously agreed to permit Ashley to leave her bags in the motel office.

"If you want to go to the beach or pool," said P.J., "you might want to take a bathing suit."

"I'm wearing it already," said Ashley. She thanked the motel manager, and headed down the street with P.J. She felt better already.

FOUR

Gaffer's Miscalculation

Captain Billy emerged from his cabin a bit shaky but not too badly hung over, and in a fair mood considering the abuse he had given his body the previous night. At about noon he took over the helm, and the anglers continued fishing until 3:00 PM. A total of five wahoos were iced down in the fish box. The last catch was a nice one, probably big enough to keep the team in first place. As they set out for the hour return ride to Bimini, Gaffer cleaned the three smallest wahoos and stored the steaks in the freezer. When that was done, he tidied up the cockpit area, putting away the tackle and washing down the cleaning tray and cockpit deck. By the time he was finished with these few chores, *Fearless Flyer* was slowing down for the no wake zone at the entrance to Bimini harbor.

The golf cart was parked at the edge of the pine trees on the bluff overlooking Bimini's Half Mile Beach. P.J. had borrowed the cart from Captain Jake in return for a promise to trade off some of *Fearless Flyer's* wahoo steaks. P.J. figured that was a promise he would somehow be able to keep.

P.J. stepped into the water only up to his ankles. Being a Florida boy, he usually waited until around May, when the water temp averaged around eighty degrees. This was November, and the ocean was eight to ten degrees too cold for him. On the other hand, Ashley was from Denver and the water felt just fine to her. She took a running start from the beach and dived head first into the water. She came up gasping, not having realized that the water could be fifteen degrees colder than the air surrounding it. P.J. sat on the beach blanket and laughed as Ashley bolted from the water shivering and covered in goose bumps. He handed her a towel which she immediately used to wipe the cold water from her skin. She then wrapped herself in the beach towel and sat on the blanket along side P.J.

True to his image of himself, P.J. produced a cigar from his backpack and lit it. Ashley looked at him oddly but said nothing. After watching him take in the acrid smoke and nearly gag on it, Ashley asked, "Aren't you going to offer me one?"

P.J. was startled. Could she mean it? He rummaged through his backpack and produced his last cigar, a ragtag looking thing that had probably left the docks in Cuba two years earlier, and had sat on the shelf of one of the small Bimini shops since that time. It was stiff and stale, and when he lit the end of it for her, smoke came not only from the tip, but also from two pin holes along the side. If Ashley were to smoke the cigar, she would have to hold her fingers over the holes, something like playing a flute. She took several puffs off the smelly tobacco roll. P.J. watched her and crinkled his nose. Ashley saw him looking at her.

"Is something wrong?" she asked.

"A cigar doesn't look right sticking out of your lips," said P.J. "There's something out of place about it."

"Really? And how do you think you look with one?"

P.J. was dumbfounded. He had not thought about that. **He** was only trying to act cool. "You tell me," he said.

Ashley took the cigar from her lips and spit on the ground. She tossed the ratty tasting thing into the ocean. "I'll just say that you don't look as cool as you probably are," she said. "Oh yeah, and another thing, I was thinking we might have an opportunity for a kiss before this day ended. But, I don't think that's going to happen now. Your breath probably smells like something scraped off the floor of a barn."

P.J. did not know which of her statements to take first. That was a mouth full. Wisely he took his time to think about what had just been said and he organized his thoughts. A minute later he believed he had a solution, something that would move this relationship ahead and overcome the dumb image building behavior that had so badly backfired. Again he rummaged through his backpack. He found a small plastic dispenser, half full of Tic-Tacs. He stood and walked over to the shoreline and tossed his cigar into the ocean. He then popped a half dozen of the mints into his mouth and offered the dispenser to Ashley. She accepted and tossed two into her mouth. Immediately her mouth tasted much better. P.J. knelt on the blanket next to Ashley and said "Now, how about that kiss."

Ashley looked fondly at P.J. and smiled. She moved closer to him and placed her hand on his shoulder. She came within a few inches of his face and said, "Much better, P.J. Maybe later."

P.J.'s shoulders sagged and his face showed the disappointment. No kiss, then why did he throw his cigar into the ocean? Embarrassed by being what he considered rejected, P.J. lay on the beach blanket facing away from Ashley. He knew the story; this is the price he paid for giving in to his need to have an image of something he was not, and for being too forward with a girl he had just met. He deserved what he got.

Five minutes later Ashley suggested, "Do you think we should go?"

P.J. sat back on his elbows looking out to sea. "We just got **here**. Are you sure you want to leave?"

"It feels so awkward. Are you mad at me?"

It was P.J.'s opportunity for redemption. He looked at her and gave that killer smile, "No way. I was an ass and you called me on it. If you can forgive me for acting that way, I can easily forget the whole thing. In fact, I'd like to forget the whole thing."

"Then it's forgotten," said Ashley.

They lay around on the blanket for another half hour. The sun was past its zenith and the beach had become quite warm. Ashley felt it was time to cool off again in the water. P.J. decided to brave it with her. After the first minute of cold water shock, it became bearable and P.J. and Ashley spent ten minutes, first swimming, then trying to float on their backs. Cooled by the chilly water they returned to the blanket and toweled off.

"This part of Bimini is like paradise," said Ashley. "If you close your eyes you can imagine being on a remote tropical island."

P.J. looked at her quizzically. "You know, Ashley, if you open your eyes you'll see that you are on a remote tropical island."

Ashley opened her eyes and looked around. She burst into laughter as she realized that he was right. P.J. was caught up in Ashley's contagious laughter and joined her for a chuckle.

"Our three hours are up. It's time to think about finding a place for you to stay," said P.J. "But first, let's stop by Sea Crest and get your stuff."

Ashley agreed. They gathered up the beach blanket and towels and headed back up to the golf cart. They rode back to Sea Crest Marina and returned Jake's cart. From there they walked across the street and retrieved Ashley's suitcase. Fifteen minutes later they were mounting the stairs to the second floor snack bar of the Big Game Club where P.J. ordered a coke for himself and a ginger ale for Ashley. As they downed their soft drinks, *Fearless Flyer* idled up to the marina.

When P.J. saw them coming, he walked over to the broad sliding glass doors and stepped out onto the balcony overlooking the marina. "That's my father and brother," he said to Ashley. "They're on that boat right there." He pointed down to where *Fearless Flyer* had just come into view. Ashley joined P.J. on the balcony. There was a lot of activity with boats docking and fishermen gathering around the scales to watch the weigh-in.

Gaffer followed his father up the ladder and onto the bridge. "I called in to the tournament committee," said Max. "So far we only need thirty pounds to stay in the lead. I'd say we have nearly a hundred."

"How many more boats need to weigh in?" asked Billy.

"Most of them," answered Max. When he saw the disappointed look on the Captain's face he added, "Listen, Billy, the chances of maintaining the lead and winning the tournament are pretty slim at best. I wouldn't start spending that prize money yet. One or two days in the lead is a long way from the finish line."

"I know that," said Billy. "But it's nice to be winning."

"Oh, yeah. You're definitely a force to be reckoned with. That kind of thing doesn't go unnoticed. And that hundred and twelve pounder will also be noticed."

Billy slowed to idle speed and then went to neutral. When the props were no longer spinning, he shifted into reverse to halt the boat's forward momentum. *Fearless Flyer* was stopped in the water. It needed to be brought into the middle of the marina basin, turned at a ninety degree angle and lined up with the slip. There was no wind or current.

An idea came to Gaffer. "Billy, can I dock the boat. I could use the practice. I park my boat all the time, but I don't get that many chances to dock bigger boats." *Fearless Flyer* was a forty-six foot long, thirteen foot wide Hatteras. It had four controls; a gear shift for each engine and a throttle for each. Only a skilled boat operator should try docking it. Gaffer's experience was in docking *Bimini Twist*, a twenty-six foot open fisherman with twin outboards. It had only two controls, as each acted as gear and throttle control for an engine. Maneuvering *Fearless Flyer* was altogether different.

Billy nodded his approval. Max moved toward the ladder. "I'll get the dock lines," he said. That was normally Gaffer's job, but since Gaffer was going to be extremely busy, Max stood in for him in the cockpit and on the deck. When the Dock Master saw *Fearless Flyer* coming, he mounted his bicycle and peddled out to the slip. He would hand the lines across to Max as soon as the boat was in position.

Things went badly for Gaffer from the outset. While he understood the basics of how to line a boat up to its slip and ease it in, his lack of experience with the multiple controls became immediately evident. When he placed the port transmission forward and the starboard into reverse, everything was fine for the first ten seconds. The stern began moving around nicely as the bow swung opposite. In fact, the bow swung too far around and Gaffer meant to correct by moving the starboard transmission gear shift lever to neutral which meant moving it forward. That would have been the correct solution. But Gaffer was confused, and moved the throttle lever forward instead of the transmission lever. Instead of going gently to neutral, the boat rocked violently ahead and swung far too much to port. Gaffer immediately saw his mistake and panicked. Instead of throttling down and attempting to correct with the starboard throttle in reverse, he threw the gear shift lever into reverse. Now the boat was backing down at far too great a speed and headed straight for a tall wooden piling the size of a telephone pole. Billy sprang to the controls and placed both transmissions into neutral, and then shifted the port transmission into forward. The starboard engine revved to 2,500 RPM's in neutral making a loud noise, while a much worse sound emerged from the rear of the boat as its swim platform connected with the wooden piling. It was the swim platform that gave in, leaving hardly a scratch on the piling. Billy wrestled the boat under control and had it standing still at a diagonal to the slip. All that was left to do was for Max, Gaffer, and the anglers to go out on the deck and push the boat around by hand until it was lined up with the slip, and then to ease it into its parking space using the controls the correct way.

Gaffer's heart was in his throat for making such a bonehead mistake. In all his years of docking boats, nothing like this had ever happened. He was certain he would never forget the crunching sound of the swim ladder as it cracked under the pressure of being squeezed against the piling. He looked around to see that there was a small crowd gathering to see what had happened. In addition to being humiliated for pulling such an amateur maneuver, he was sickened to think how much it was going to cost to have the platform repaired.

Gaffer could not be consoled. Billy tried to tell him that this type of thing happens to all boaters. Max also tried to calm him. Nothing made him feel any better. He opened the transom door and looked down at the swim platform. For the first time he really noticed its construction. From what he could remember from all the boat shows he had attended, the most expensive ones were made of teak and were in an open weave that water could run through like a sieve. This one looked to be more cheaply built out of two or three layers of fibre glass over wooden stringers. Billy looked over the transom with him. He patted Gaffer on the back. "You're lucky," he said.

Gaffer shook his head in disgust. His head was pounding and his stomach turned. The color had drained from his face. "I sure don't feel lucky," he said.

"Well, take my word for it, you are. We can repair that right here in the water with a little wood, and fibre glass, and some paint. I'll show you how."

"It looks pretty messed up to me," said Gaffer. "Are you sure we can fix it?"

"It looks worse than it is," said Billy. "I'm sure." Those words gave Gaffer some comfort, and he soon began to calm down. He tried to take his mind off the damage by jumping ashore and getting the wheelbarrow so he and his team could join the weigh-in.

The crowd surrounding the scales was beginning to grow. It seemed that every captain who showed up with his entry had fish larger

44

than the ones that had gone before. Billy and Gaffer hoisted their entries onto the scales. The results were gratifying with a forty-five pound fish, and the third largest fish of the day, weighing in at sixty-two pounds. It was a good total, but two other boats beat them. *Sea Eagle* moved into third place overall, ten pounds behind *Fearless Flyer*. *Snuggle Bear* moved into first place, fifteen pounds ahead of Captain Billy.

Gaffer looked around and saw P.J. standing behind him. "Hey, Bro. How's it going?"

P.J. shrugged. "Pretty good, I guess."

"Did you see what I did?" asked Gaffer.

"You mean the part where the boat met the piling?"

"Oh," said Gaffer, "you saw it."

"Yeah," said P.J. "Nice work."

"Thanks." Gaffer saw that P.J. was with someone. He leaned forward to get a better look.

"Hi," said Ashley.

"Hi. I'm Gaffer."

Ashley extended her hand, "I'm please to meet you. I'm Ashley."

Gaffer showed her his filthy hand wearing a sun glove and covered in wahoo blood and slime. "I don't think you want to shake this hand," he said. "I'll catch you later on that one."

Ashley giggled and wrinkled her nose. "It's nice to meet you." As she looked over at the scales, Gaffer checked her out better. He looked at his brother and raised his eyebrows. P.J. shrugged. It was the silent language they understood. Gaffer was acknowledging that P.J. had found a beauty. P.J.'s shrug meant he knew it.

Max came out of the crowd and saw P.J. "Hey, Peej, how was

your day? Did you get any studying done? " He decided to back off. P.J. always thought his father was grilling him when he asked about studies. He finally settled for, "How's it going?"

P.J. steered his father aside. "Dad, I have a friend here who needs a place to stay. She came here with a guy who's being real obnoxious with her, trying to make her do things she didn't bargain for. Any way we can help her? She's really stuck."

Ashley returned to where P.J. was standing. He introduced her to his father. They traded courteous greetings. Max nodded to P.J. "We'll figure something out."

P.J. turned to Ashley. "You're covered. My dad will help."

Ashley looked relieved. "That's great," she said. To Max she said, "Thank you, Mr. Carson. That's a real relief."

"Of course," said Max. "Don't worry about a thing. We'll make sure you're OK."

The weigh-in crowd soon began to disperse. Gaffer was at the cleaning table making steaks out of one hundred seven pounds of wahoos. P.J. followed his father down to the slip where *Fearless Flyer* was docked. "Dad, do you think we could get Ashley settled? She's been without a room all day."

Max addressed Ashley, "You have a couple of choices," he said. "I know there are rooms available here. I'd be glad to rent one for you if you like. The other choice is you can stay on the boat. The only problem with that is that we only have a couch for you to sleep on and we leave early in the morning for fishing. If you chose the boat, you can either go with us, or get up early and stay ashore until we return."

Ashley did not have to think twice about the offer. "I have a choice of staying in a room by myself up there," pointing to the area where the motel rooms were located, "or I can stay on this cool boat with you guys and have company and people to talk with." She rolled her eyes. "I appreciate both offers; I'll bunk on the boat."

"OK," said Max. "That's fine. P.J., take Ashley's things on board and show her where the showers are."

"The boat shower or the one on shore?"

"I think she'll be more comfortable on shore, the water heater on board isn't heating that well."

P.J. helped Ashley across to the cockpit and showed her **around** the boat. They found a spot in the crew's cabin where she could store her belongings. After she settled in she gathered her toiletries and some clean clothes and headed out to the showers.

Curt Sikes treated the entire group, including the anglers, Billy Bray, Ashley and the Carsons to dinner at the Anchorage. The sun was setting over the horizon and the gulls were gently spiraling around on currents of air. It was a pristine setting, a suitable ending to a good day. Ashley asked P.J. and Gaffer to follow her outside. There she produced a pocket camera and made certain every combination of the group had their picture taken. P.J. with Ashley, P.J. with Gaffer, Ashley with Gaffer, and then she asked a young boy who happened to be passing by, to get a picture of the three of them. Finally she had P.J. take her picture with the young boy.

At 9:00 PM Gaffer was fighting sleep. His food came and he devoured it, but he was finding it very difficult to sit around waiting for everyone else to finish. He told his father that he was really beat and asked if he could be excused to return to the boat. He said good night to everyone, thanked Curt for his hospitality, and twenty minutes later was asleep in his bunk.

An hour later P.J. and Ashley were sitting in the cockpit looking at the stars and unwinding from the activities of the day. Max and Billy were in the salon going over last minute plans for tomorrow's competition, studying the tides and currents, checking the weather forecast, and generally making certain everything was ready for the last day of the tournament. They were well poised to win the tournament, and they wanted to maximize those possibilities to the extent they could. An hour later the lights went out and everyone was passed out in their beds. They had earned a good night's sleep.

FIVE

Dream Machine

The wind picked up during the night. By sunup it was blowing a steady twenty knots directly out of the north. Today's optimum tide would be at 12:32 PM, meaning there was no hurry to put the lines in the water. With the rule being that the lines had to come out of the water by 4:00 PM, and the fish to be weighed by 5:00, there was little reason for *Fearless Flyer* to leave the dock before 10:00 AM. So it **was a** leisurely morning with most of the crew beginning to stir at 7:30 AM, and moving aimlessly about the boat for the first hour. Ashley was up and raring to go.

Gaffer had moved quietly through the salon and was already in the cockpit making sure his tackle was in top condition for the day. All these preparations had to be completed before the boat left the dock. There would be no chance of getting this work done on the **rocking** deck after they left the marina. Ashley joined Gaffer in the cock**pit and** bade him a good morning. They exchanged pleasantries, talked about how nice the weather was, and how cool Bimini was. Ashley was curious about what Gaffer was doing. It was a surprise to her that good **rigs** had to be made, that they didn't come in a box ready to be snapped onto the end of the line. Gaffer twisted and crimped, and replaced any frayed shock cords and bent snap swivels. He examined the last hundred feet of wire for any kinks that might cause the line to separate.

49

"You're really fussy about your hooks and knots, aren't you?" asked Ashley.

"I have a huge responsibility for this equipment," said Gaffer. "These anglers paid good money to compete in this tournament, and I need to make sure that they get every possible chance to win. That means I have to be as careful as I know how when it comes **to the** equipment and following the rules. This is my first tournament as a paid mate with a possibility of some prize money. I not only want everything to go perfectly, I also want to place. That way more boats will **want** to hire me for the tournaments."

"I see you're motivated," said Ashley.

Gaffer nodded. "Highly."

"So, what's it like out there when you fish?"

"Yesterday was awesome, a beautiful day. The day before was really snotty, but that's the day we caught the hundred and twelve pounder. You just never know."

"Isn't it dangerous?" asked Ashley.

"I wouldn't call it dangerous, but I would say there are opportunities to make mistakes, and there are chances to get hurt. But they're all minimized if you're careful and you know what you're doing."

"Do you think I'd like it?"

Gaffer looked at Ashley and flinched. She appeared high maintenance, nicely groomed, well manicured, perhaps a bit frail, and not the least bit athletic. "It's hard to say. But days out there like today, where the wind is blowing out of the north, are usually pretty ugly. You might have been OK yesterday, but I don't think today would be too good for you."

"P.J. tells me he gets seasick. Don't you?"

"I have a stomach for it. I've been on the ocean most of **my** life and I don't feel it that much. Sometimes when we're headed down wind and the diesel exhaust is blowing in my face, I get a little queasy. In truth, I really prefer the motion of a smaller boat. But I haven't **ever** chummed, if that's what you mean."

"I have," said Ashley. "It's not fun."

"I don't think today would be the right day for you. I can already tell from the wind that it's going to be rough."

That was the end of Ashley's interest in wahoo fishing **for this** day. "Good luck," she said. "I'm going back inside."

Gaffer stopped her. "If you want to make yourself useful, there's a way you can help."

That sounded good to her. "Sure, what can I do?"

"Well, everybody's still in slow gear in there," he said, nodding to the salon. "In a little while they'll be trying to get around, all going in different directions. You could help to get the galley started. Cou**ld you** make a pot of coffee, or some toast or something?"

"Absolutely," said Ashley. "I'd love to."

She moved inside and began familiarizing herself with the galley. She was well trained in kitchen arts and soon the smells of breakfast wafted throughout the boat. One by one the men finished up in the head and moved toward the salon. Gaffer came back inside within fifteen minutes and joined the others. Ashley had done a good job of getting the crew focused on the new day.

P.J. was moving slowly, but was alert enough to know that he would be getting off the boat before it left the dock. He hurriedly finished his breakfast and took care of his grooming in the head. He packed a small backpack with the things he thought he might need for a day ashore. The party of anglers boarded the boat and Curt Sikes again handed P.J. his room key. It wasn't long before *Fearless Flyer* was idling out of the marina, and P.J. was on the dock winding up lines and the shore power cord. He was glad to be on solid ground.

The first line hit the water at 11:00. For the fourth day in a row Captain Billy had selected the area off Gun Cay Cut at the 400 foot level. This spot had produced well enough to keep them in second place, so why change what was working? In five to seven foot seas Gaffer let the two lines run out and locked up the reels. He climbed half way up the ladder so Billy could hear him. "Let me know if you see any weeds on the line or if I have to check them. I can't see past the wake."

Billy gave the thumbs up. Gaffer would know if a wahoo hit; the line would scream off the reel and the clicker would sound like a low-pitched siren. But the choppy seas made it impossible to watch the line from the cockpit. He would just have to rely on Billy to let him know if the lines needed attending for other reasons.

From the moment the lines went into the water, Gaffer and his anglers were expecting a hit. That was the way it always was with fishermen in these tournaments. A strike could come at any time, and so a high level of alertness took over as soon as the lines went out. The cockpit deck was wet and slippery. It pitched and rolled, creating conditions that would make most people seasick. Gaffer preferred to call it an 'interesting' sea.

Twenty minutes into the set Gaffer was startled when Captain

Billy throttled down. He walked back to where he could see the **captain**. "What's up?" he called.

Billy looked frantic. He pointed to the west and called down. "Wind 'em up! I just heard a may-day from *Dream Machine*. A minute later I saw all that black smoke on the horizon. Can you see it?"

Gaffer did not answer, he was already reeling in the port line; Max had the one on starboard. "Don't wait for us. These lines will be in before you can get up to speed. Take off!"

Billy pushed the throttles to the wall. Heading west he had a beam sea, so *Fearless Flyer* rocked and rolled, but made excellent time. It covered the three miles in fifteen minutes and was the first boat on site. There was not another minute to spare as flames had engulfed the entire super structure of the yacht and the crew and passengers stood in their cockpit in water up to the gunwales, hoping to be rescued before the boat went down. Six crew and passengers stood in the hip deep water wearing their life jackets, and tied to each other with nylon ropes. The group on *Fearless Flyer* were also now wearing life jackets, and readying themselves for the rescue.

Max turned to see Billy half way down the ladder. "Go back up," he said. "Someone needs to drive the boat. It's under control down here. Back up as close as you can, and I'll toss the life-ring over. We'll take the passengers one at a time."

Billy was impressed to see that everyone on his boat was also wearing life jackets. Max had the ring in his right hand and the end of the line tied to it in his left. He was ready to let fly. He had already **called** over to the other boat and told its occupants what to expect. Wave**s and** sea spray had doused the fire, and there no longer appeared to be a danger of explosion. But they were running out of time as the boat was two thirds submerged, and any one of the next waves might finish the job.

Max and Gaffer looked in horror at the carnage to the yacht. It was a sixty-three foot Garlington; a $3,000,000 boat. Now it listed to port at a forty-five degree angle like a dying behemoth, being tossed helplessly around, giving in to every motion of the overbearing sea. All around were floating remembrances of the luxury yacht it had been. Boat cushions, ice chests, towels, papers, and just about anything else that could float, mixed in with the diesel fuel that had created a slick the size of a football field. It was a terrible scene that none of the rescue party would ever forget. High seas, wind and waves, and helpless passengers whose remaining hope was to get out of this situation **alive**. All hope for what had been the beautiful and graceful *Dream Machine* was lost.

The passengers were going to have to enter the water. At this point, the sinking boat was more a threat to safety than it was a refuge. Max instructed them to get into the water and kick toward *Fearless Flyer*.

Reluctantly the first person floated away from the cockpit of the sinking boat. One by one the others followed. It was a difficult and dangerous situation. Diesel fuel stung their eyes and the waves **tossed** them. Their foresight to tie themselves together proved to be **wise,** as they had little control over the direction of their movements once they hit the open water.

The first of the group was holding on to the life ring and **being** hauled toward the rescue boat by Max and Gaffer. Billy backed **down on** the group and cut in half the distance between where they entered the water and his own position. Every bit would help. After what seemed like an eternity of hauling, the first passenger was at the swim platform. Gaffer saw that it was a woman. She was shivering violently and had used all of her strength in grasping the life ring. She was about to let go when Curt Sikes yelled at her fiercely. "Lady, hold on another few seconds. We're going to haul you in on the next wave. Get ready!" He saw what he thought was an almost imperceptible nod.

Max and Gaffer turned their attention to the rest of the heads bobbing in the water. Another life ring was tossed out and they were working with the next person in line. In no time at all, perhaps a second or two, the next wave was there. As the lady rose with the wave, Curt and his nephew, Denny, grabbed her life jacket and hauled her in. She slid through the transom door and onto the deck. Denny stood by to stop her from colliding with the fighting chair or any of the other objects protruding from the floor of the cockpit. He wanted to stand her up as quickly as possible. When she was on her feet, Denny untied the nylon rope holding her to the rest of the group. While he helped her out of the life jacket, Gaffer wrapped the end of the cord to a cleat, thus anchoring the rest of the group to the boat.

The woman was nearly hypothermic. By the time she was standing on the deck, she had been in the water for twenty minutes The color had drained from her skin, she was shivering violently, and she was nearly in shock.

Max said to Denny, "Use the hose to wash her off. That water is warmer than the sea water by twenty degrees. Get the salt off her, give her some towels to dry off, and find her some dry clothes. There are plenty of blankets inside. Make sure she is dry and wrapped in blankets."

Then Gaffer and Curt hauled the second survivor aboard quite easily. As the third member of the party floated through the transom door, the line between the fourth and fifth person came untied, separating him and the man behind him from the main body of the group.

Max was washing down the men as they came aboard, showering off salt water and diesel fuel. The outdoor shower felt good on the survivors' skin, it cleansed them and gently warmed them. Denny was inside the cabin finding towels, clothing, and blankets for the new arrivals.

Jump-In, another contestant in the tournament, was the only other boat to answer the may-day. As soon as Captain Mack Ritchie heard the call, he too turned to the west and pushed the throttle to full. It was fortunate that he did, because he was on site when the two men had become separated from the original line. Before Billy could back around and run to them, Mack was lining up to bring them onboard his vessel. But *Jump In* was dangerously close to *Fearless Flyer*. Only twenty feet separated the vessels, and this distance could be covered by a single wave with one bad bit of luck.

"I've got them," called Captain Ritchie. "But I need to maneuver. I need you out of the way."

Billy called across, "I'm moving. Don't worry about me. Just keep doing what you're doing."

But Mack was not listening. He was using all of his concentration to line up on the two men in the water. He knew *Fearless Flyer* was dangerously close, but even if the wave action caused them to bump against each other, it would not be a serious collision. They might lose some paint or take out a rail, but the business of rescuing these two survivors was much too important to be worrying about collateral damage.

Fearless Flyer was positioned bow into the waves. With the wind and waves pushing it to the south, it was easy to go into reverse with both engines, and slip neatly away from the other boat. Once he had moved the first ten feet away, the next fifty feet was easy. In only a few seconds more *Fearless Flyer* was sitting at idle, a hundred feet away from *Jump-In*, and in no danger of colliding. Billy watched the action as it unfolded. Max climbed the first two steps toward the bridge.

"It's under control below," he said. "The first survivor, the lady, is now in dry clothes and wrapped in blankets. The others have all been washed down with fresh water and we're in the process of finding dry clothes and blankets for them."

"What about injuries?" asked Billy.

"Yes, a couple of them will need a doctor. No doubt."

"How many of them are there?"

"There are four on board," said Max. "There were a total of six."

Billy looked around at the wind tossed sea. The slick of diesel fuel and floating debris had dissipated and now covered an area a half mile square. He called Captain Ritchie on the VHS. "Let me be clear, you have two survivors on board. Is that correct?"

"That's a ten-four," came the response.

Billy waved across to *Jump-In's* bridge. This was good. He keyed the microphone again, "We have four. That means all the survivors have been rescued."

"OK," came the response.

"Are any of your passengers injured or need a doctor?"

"That's affirmative," said Mack. "One has been temporarily blinded by the fuel in the water. He banged his shoulder getting on my boat. I don't know how bad that is. The other has burns on his face and arm."

"Ten-four," said Billy. "We have some injuries here too. I'm going to radio ahead to Bimini for the doctor to be standing by at the dock."

"We could take them to Miami where they could be admitted to a real hospital if you think we should," said Mack.

"In this sea that's a four hour trip," called back Billy. "Bimini will take an hour. If anyone needs to go to the hospital we can call a chopper from there. It'll still be faster. Are your passengers' injuries that bad?"

"I don't know," came the response. "For right now we'll make them comfortable and see how things look when we get into port."

"Ten-four," called Billy. "*Fearless Flyer*, out."

"*Jump-In*, out."

Simultaneously the men pushed the throttles on their boats to the wall and took a heading of thirty degrees. After ten minutes of running Billy called over to Captain Ritchie, "Is everything under control? How are your passengers?"

"Better," replied Mac. "We gave some eye drops to the guy who was blinded and he's doing better. I'm worried for the guy with the burns. He seems to have a lot of pain."

"Burns are bad," said Billy. "I hope he's OK. I called ahead. The doctor will be at the Big Game Club dock when we arrive."

"Ten-four."

In the distance Billy could see the entrance to Bimini Harbour. His new passengers huddled in the salon, wrapped in blankets and sipping on hot tea. Gaffer headed back out to the cockpit and started up the ladder. Billy saw him there and called down, "Is everyone OK?"

Gaffer came up to the bridge. "Everyone's fine. They're all dry and wrapped up. The woman is just beginning to get comfortable."

"Did they tell you how the fire started?"

"A propane gas bottle was leaking and there was an explosion."

"Bummer."

Boats rocked in the marinas along the Bimini waterfront as *Fearless Flyer* and *Jump-In* cruised into the Big Game Club way too fast. It was an unusual circumstance; they had injured passengers who needed immediate attention, and there was an emergency crew waiting for them. The trip in had taken only forty minutes as both boats returned to port at full throttle. By this time the condition of the survivors had been positively determined. The burn victim was the yacht's owner. It appeared that his forearm had received a third degree burn. The burns on his face were superficial, but painful just the same.

The woman was the owner's wife. She had recovered from the exposure and was comfortable. However she was nearly hysterical worrying about her husband on the other boat. They spoke on the VHS several times during the ride into Bimini. The husband tried hard to be stoic and not allow her to worry excessively. Nevertheless, she was most anxious to get to his side as soon as they arrived in port.

The yacht's captain traveled with the owner's wife aboard *Fearless Flyer*. He was having trouble moving his left arm. Sharp pain radiated from his shoulder when he moved it. He also could not put weight on his left ankle. It was either severely sprained, or possibly broken. The man whose eyes were badly irritated by the diesel fuel in the water had already fully recovered. All of the other survivors seemed to be in good shape.

A crowd gathered at the dock as Billy and Mack parked their boats. Gently the survivors were brought ashore. The more badly injured of them were immediately attended. The yacht's owner and its captain were taken by stretcher to the nearby clinic. The other two survivors walked off under their own steam.

CHAPTER SIX

The Diamonds

The celebration of the weigh-in was insignificant compared to the stir created by the rescue. Captains Billy and Mack were elevated to folk hero status the moment the first survivor walked across to the Big Game Club dock. When the physician hurried into the marina, he was followed by the town's two full time constables. The parade, coupled with the buzz around the island on telephones and VHS radios, created a shockwave that drew a crowd. Two hundred people milled around the dock waiting for the two boats to return. In typical Bimini style, when the survivors touched land, the pool bar opened and the rum began to flow.

Dream Machine's owner, Jeremy Diamond, a real estate broker and developer from Coral Gables, Florida, along with his wife, Jessica, and Captain Jimmy Pile, were rushed to the medical clinic two blocks north of the Big Game Club. In a matter of minutes their injuries were being treated. When cleaned up and dressed it was determined that the worst part of Mr. Diamond's burns covered only an area five inches square. His facial burns were no worse than a bad sunburn. He considered himself fortunate as these injuries could have been much worse. Captain Pile's shoulder was found to be dislocated. It was placed back in its socket in a very jarring and painful procedure. An xray showed that there was no break in his ankle, and an ice pack was applied.

Jessica Diamond used the clinic's telephone to arrange for a helicopter to pick up the party while Jeremy was assisted by the Chief Constable in filling out a dozen official forms relating to the sunken vessel, the injured individuals, and the usual customs and immigration forms for departing visitors. It would be two hours before the helicopter would land, so Jeremy and Jessica Diamond made their way back to the Big Game Club while Jimmy Pile stayed at the clinic with his ankle packed in ice.

Fearless Flyer was docked in its berth two slips over from *Jump-In*. The crews of both boats were performing their clean ups as the couple walked slowly toward them. In addition to the usual fresh water wash down, both boats needed to be scrubbed down with a strong grease cutting solvent to remove the diesel fuel from the sides and transoms. There was also the extra work associated with airing out wet carpeting and furniture. When the Diamonds approached, Max Carson was working in the cockpit of *Fearless Flyer*, wiping the windows and fighting chair with chamois.

Jeremy Diamond stood on the dock and hailed him. "Hello there," he called.

Max looked up from what he was doing. He immediately recognized the man and climbed onto the dock. Mr. Diamond's face was shiny with burn medicine and his arm was bandaged from his elbow to his wrist, but other than that he looked pretty good considering what he had endured earlier in the day. The color had returned to Mrs. Diamond's face and she had brushed her hair. Beyond that, she had no chance to apply makeup, so Max was seeing her as few people ever did, naturally. But she was a nice looking woman, probably quite beautiful when fully made up. Gaffer's hooded sweater was many sizes too large for her.

Max extended his hand and introduced himself to Jeremy Diamond. Jessica also shook his hand and thanked him for the hundredth time for saving their lives. Max called Captain Billy over to meet Mr. Diamond. It was Billy who was knocked out of the competition for having answered the may-day. Max wanted to subtly make sure the Diamonds understood that.

Billy invited the Diamonds aboard *Fearless Flyer* for a relaxing cocktail while they waited for their ride to arrive at the airport. Max and Gaffer joined them as the work of cleaning the boat was nearly complete, and it was getting too dark to see what they were doing anyhow.

"My sweatshirt looks good on you," said Gaffer with a broad smile.

Jessica Diamond smiled. "You're a dear. I'll have it cleaned and be sure it makes its way back to you."

"No need," said Gaffer. "You're welcome to it."

"Can I pay you for it?" she asked.

"Not a chance," said Gaffer. "You have no idea how good I feel, how good we all feel, that you and your party are safe, and that we were able to be a part of it."

"That's the truth," said Captain Billy. "I mean, we're sorry for your lost boat, and your injuries. That's tragic. But we have to admit that we're all lucky to be sitting here like this now. This could have ended a dozen different ways. This was not too bad."

"We're alive and thankful," said Mrs. Diamond. "The boat is just iron and glass and can be replaced." She paused as tears welled up in her eyes. With emotion that only a traumatic near death experience can create she choked out, "Lives can not be replaced."

There was a half minute of silence in the salon as Mrs. Diamond composed herself and everyone else thought about her words. The pause was for a moment of reflection about the gift of life that is so often taken for granted. The reverie was broken as Captain Mack Ritchie slid open the door to the salon and entered with his first mate. He and the mate were introduced to Jessica Diamond who stood and hugged them both in gratitude for saving her husband and Jimmy Pile.

"I'm the kind of guy who likes to reward people for their kindnesses. And I owe you people my life. How do I repay that?"

"You already said thank you," said Max. "That's all I need."

"I'm good with that too," said Gaffer.

"Me too," said Billy. "Seeing you and your wife here, safe and alive does it for me."

Mack Ritchie and his first mate nodded their agreement.

"By the way," said Max, "How's your captain?"

"I think he'll recover quickly," said Jeremy. "He had a dislocated shoulder that has been repositioned. The doctor says it'll be OK. He has a badly sprained ankle that will keep him immobile for a few days."

"The other passengers looked pretty good the last time I saw them," said Billy.

"Yes, they're fine," said Jessica. "That's my brother and two of the men who work in Jeremy's office."

"Where are they?" asked Max. "I haven't seen them since we docked."

Jessica pointed to the upstairs lounge. "Up there having **a todd**y to calm their nerves, and enjoying the view."

The conversation continued for another hour. It was light and friendly. Soon enough the sun sank behind the Queens Highway ridge and its glow began to fade. The Diamonds had to excuse themselves to collect the rest of their party for the trip down to the heli-pad. Mrs. Diamond made certain she had the names, addresses and telephone numbers of the crews from *Fearless Flyer* and *Jump-In*. It was obvious that she intended to reward them in some way for having saved them **earlier** in the day.

Max borrowed three golf carts from the Big Game Club. Gaffer quickly buzzed over to the clinic and collected Jimmy Pile. He assisted him onto the seat and then spun around to pick up Mr. and **Mrs.** Diamond. The three other men were already on Max's golf cart **ready** to go when Gaffer arrived. They headed down the road single file, Max behind Gaffer, followed by Mack Ritchie's cart.

Max and Gaffer didn't know much about helicopters, but **when** they saw this one settling in for a landing, they knew it was one **of the** fancy ones. It had a pilot and co-pilot and it looked to have about twelve passenger seats. There was some kind of turbo thruster that would make it go two hundred miles an hour. It was sleek and expensive looking**, and** on the tail was the logo of one of the major fast food chains. It app**eared** that the Diamonds had some very wealthy friends.

The survivors lined up to hug and shake hands with the crews that had saved them. They were a ragtag looking group, wearing a **variety** of clothing that had been scrounged from the two rescue boats. **Max saw** his favorite windbreaker go by as well as a pair of shorts he did not care too much about, and an old pair of deck shoes that he had been meaning to replace, but to which he felt attached, as P.J. had given them to him for Father's Day two years earlier. He shrugged and let them go. Gaffer watched his sweatshirt go as well as his best Bimini Twist tee shirt. He flinched as his well-worn flip flops that he had owned for as long as his feet had grown to size twelve, walked away. The rest of the crews from *Fearless Flyer* and *Jump-In* went through similar experiences as they watched parts of their wardrobes climb aboard the helicopter.

But everyone was feeling good about themselves. The Diamonds seemed like very nice people, very appreciative for the sacrifices that both crews had made. The crews knew that they may have saved lives and felt very good about that. A major luxury yacht had met its fate this day. That was a shame and a waste. Riding back in the golf cart with his father, Gaffer was philosophical.

"I heard what Mrs. Diamond said about the yacht being only iron and glass. It's hard to believe she could see it that way. They must have spent millions on that boat."

"I'm sure they did," said Max. "But what's that in comparison to people's lives. She was probably thinking she could have lost her husband or her brother in that accident. They can always buy a new yacht. They probably will. But her life would never be the same if someone had died when the boat went down."

"But still, the boat," said Gaffer.

"It's just iron and glass," replied his father.

When the golf carts returned to the Big Game Club, the party was raging. The prizes had been awarded. Through some stroke of good fortune, Doc Strauss's *Accupleasure* had caught two monster wahoos, a ninety-two pounder and a hundred and five pounder. They took first place in the tournament. Altogether with the prize money and their share of the calcutta, they won a total of $42,000. The trophy they took home was gold with blue and red highlights and stood three feet tall. *Sea Eagle* moved into second place, not because they had the best day ever in wahoo fishing, but mainly because *Fearless Flyer* had no fish to enter for the day. Third place was awarded to a boat named *Spanky* which had not been in the running until today, but with a single day's entry of 160 pounds, they rightfully finished in the money.

The crews from *Fearless Flyer* and *Jump-In* were treated like celebrities when they arrived at the party. The awards were interrupted so that several dignitaries, including the most distinguished citizens of Bimini, took turns at the microphone in congratulating the heros and recognizing them for sacrificing their chance to win a serious jackpot to answer a may-day. Curt Sikes was commended for the sacrifice he had made as the man who paid all the expenses of entering the tournament and chartering *Fearless Flyer,* but giving up the chance for the grand prize. The crew and fishing party of *Jump-In* was given equal recognition. The entire rest of the evening was spent with the high spirited tournament participants crowding the heros, and putting drinks in their hands and cigars in their shirt pockets. It was exhausting to be the center of all this attention.

Gaffer felt a need to get away. His interests were other than those of the other party goers anyhow. He did not drink alcohol and he did not like to be around people who did. P.J. and Ashley felt the same, so they left the compound and headed down Kings Highway. Gaffer realized that he was starving. As busy as he had been and with all the excitement, he had not eaten since breakfast.

The streets of Alicetown were fairly empty. Winter activities in Bimini, with the exception of the Wahoo Tournament, were pretty much nonexistent. The tourist trade was down, and many of the residents who would normally mill along Kings Highway were either in their homes or at the Big Game Club party. Gaffer steered Ashley and P.J. into the Red Lion Restaurant where he knew he could always get a good meal. There were only two tables occupied out of a possible twenty, and there was only one patron sitting at the bar. The waitress was sitting at her usual perch looking bored and ignoring her customers. Gaffer walked over to her and asked for a table for three. The waitress indicated she would be right with them. It was impossible to tell why it would take a moment to seat them, as the only thing the hostess was doing was sitting on her butt smoking a cigarette. The threesome walked over to the bar and took a seat.

P.J. glanced at the man sitting at the bar and noticed that he was looking at him intently. P.J. returned the look. These two knew each other. It took no time at all as the recognition hit both of them at the same time. And simultaneously they broke into wide grins. There was no handshake, just a giant bear hug. Gaffer glanced over to see what was up and, when he recognized the man, he stood in line for his hug too.

Cameron Ford was a lieutenant in the Royal Bahamas Defense Force. The boys had met him a few years earlier right here in Bimini when they became involved in a project to assist the police to provide surveillance against a drug ring operating in the area. The following year they spent some quality time together in the Abaco Island chain. They were shocked and amazed that they could coincidentally run into each other right here.

"What brings you to Bimini?" asked Gaffer.

"Just work," said Cameron.

"No kidding. More drug smugglers?" P.J. was referring to an incident he had seen the Defense Force be involved in on another occasion. Large quantities of drugs had been moving through the area from North Bimini to Orange Cay. The Defense Force had moved in and shut down the entire operation and confiscated a quantity of cocaine worth $100,000,000 on the streets in the U.S. The Defense Force was a well-focused, crime fighting organization with many dedicated operatives like Cameron Ford.

"There have been attempts to use this area for smuggling, but it's really small time stuff, and we pretty much have it under control."

"So, is that why you're here?" asked Gaffer.

"I'm here with Chet Christy and Cecil Hunter. We're here to make an additional police presence, to augment the permanent island police force."

"Then you'll be here for a while?" asked P.J.

"Probably a few months," answered Cameron. He and P.J. had become close friends over the years. Whenever there was a gathering of the Defense Force where the Carson family had been present, Cameron and P.J. always sought each other out as they had many ideas and values in common. It was always fun for them when they were together.

"Hold on one minute," said Gaffer. "My father is not going to believe this. He's at the Big Game Club. I'm going to go get him."

"Excellent," said Cameron. "This is great."

Gaffer ran out the door. The Big Game club was no more than fifty yards up the street and he covered it in about ten seconds. Within five minutes he was walking back into the Red Lion carrying ten pounds of wahoo filets, and followed by his father. It was a joyous reunion.

"How long are you here for?" asked Cameron.

"Weather permitting we'll be heading out in the morning," replied Max. "How about you?"

"I'll be here for a while. I'm on temporary duty to augment the permanent police force on the island. Chet and Cecil are here with me."

"No kidding," said Max. "Chet and Cecil. I haven't seen them in a while."

"Well, you know, they're our two most, shall I say enthusiastic, crime fighters."

Max laughed. "Well put," he said. "Where are they?"

"I'm waiting for them now. They had to go over to South Bimini to check into a complaint over there, and then they are supposed to meet me here."

Max ordered a round of drinks from the bartender. He instructed Gaffer to give the wahoo steaks to the chef. "I'm sorry I'm only finding out now about you guys being here. I've been here for three days, Gaffer and P.J. have been here for five. We could have spent time together."

"I'm sorry, too," said Cameron. "But we have this evening."

"And we have some fresh wahoo too," said Max. "We can have at least one feast together."

"Well then, there you go," said Cameron. Changing the subject he asked, "Did you hear about the yacht that sank today?"

"I didn't hear about it," said Max, "I saw it sink. We were right there. We helped pluck the survivors out of the ocean and brought **them** back here. Our boat was one of the rescue boats."

"*Bimini Twist?*" asked Cameron.

"No, no," said Max. "The boat we're on for the tournament, *Fearless Flyer.*"

"You're on *Fearless Flyer?*" asked Cameron.

"That's us," said Max.

"Yeah," said Cameron. "I heard all about it. You're the heros."

"They make it sound like that," said Max. "But the **truth is, we** only did what anybody would do. We had to answer the may-day, and from there we just did what had to be done." Max considered for a moment and then added, "I guess to the people on *Dream Machine* you might say we're heros."

"Put it this way," said Cameron, "change places with **those** people and what would you call yourselves."

Max considered for a moment. "Yeah, I get your point."

They chatted for another twenty minutes before the door to the restaurant opened and Chet Christy and Cecil Hunter entered. For a minute their eyes could not adjust to the darkness of the room, and they did not see Cameron in the middle of the group. Then they saw him, but still did not focus on who he was speaking with. It had been **several** years since they had seen the Carsons and recognition came **slowly.** Cameron jogged their memories. When he said, "You know, the Carsons with *Bimini Twist,*" both men lit up. No hand shakes, big hugs all around, like old friends at a reunion.

The evening wore on. Cameron told Cecil and Chet about the *Fearless Flyer* rescue adventure. They knew right away what he was talking about. The conversation was very animated as the old friends brought each other up to date on what they had been doing since they last saw each other. The party feasted on wahoo, fresh vegetables and many baskets of world famous Bimini bread. They laughed and reminisced for two hours until the waitress finally asked them to leave as the restaurant was closing. They left from there and walked down the street to the Compleat Angler to continue the reunion.

What Max did not like hearing was that crime was up on the island of Bimini. Small time drug dealers were showing up, and there were a few new go-fast boats on the waterfront looking to move contraband. As soon as Cameron, or Cecil, or Chet would put one of them away, another would pop up. All small time stuff, marijuana in sixty pound bales, cocaine in five kilo packets. But it was enough to create a problem with Customs, Immigration, and the Defense Force. And after all, it was still illegal. Max made an offer that he would not do for many people.

"Guys, my boat is staying here for the next month. We brought it over a couple of weeks ago so we could fly here during the holiday break and do some fishing. It's yours if you can use it."

"That's very generous of you," said Cameron. "I may have to take you up on that offer. Where will I find the keys if we need it?"

Max explained where the boat was being kept behind a friend's house on South Bimini. "Honestly, Cameron," he said. "It's there. Use it."

It was approaching midnight when they walked up the dock to *Fearless Flyer's* slip. They agreed that this would be an excellent cigar night. They had many reasons to celebrate. Tomorrow the Defense

Force Operatives would be back on their beat, busting criminals and doing what they could to keep the good people of Bimini safe. Tomorrow *Fearless Flyer* would head back to Fort Lauderdale and that would be the end of an excellent adventure for Captain Billy and the Carsons. It was another two hours before the party broke up.

As all good things must end, Cameron, Cecil, and Chet said good buy to their friends and made their way back to their rented house on Queens Highway. One by one the group on *Fearless Flyer* found their way to their bunks and fell into bed. It had been the longest, most exhausting day any of them could remember. They slept until an hour after sunup.

SEVEN

Lighthouse Point

Fearless Flyer idled away from the Bimini Big Game Club as its passengers reminisced about the previous five bittersweet days. Among the better memories were first of all, the saving of the owners and **guests** of *Dream Machine*. No one would ever forget that. Second was the **112** pound wahoo, and being in first place in the tournament, if only for a day. They were thankful for having good anglers who appreciated the hard work Billy, Max and Gaffer were doing, and who tipped Billy **and** Gaffer generously. It was not a happy thought about being knocked **out** of the tournament on the fourth day, but that was for a good reason and there was never a regret voiced.

The crossing from Bimini to Fort Lauderdale was rough but not dangerous. Seas of six feet off the starboard beam caused *Fearless Flyer* to rock side-to-side. It had no problem making headway and cleared the Hillsboro Inlet in three and a half hours. P.J. and Ashley became seasick during the first hour and chose to complete the crossing lying **on the** floor of the salon to minimize the motion.

When Captain Billy backed into his slip in the Lighthouse Point Yacht Club he could not have been more surprised. There, standing on the dock to catch the lines, were Jeremy and Jessica Diamond. **Mr.** Diamond's bandaged arm was hidden by the windbreaker he was wearing. His face looked a reddish brown, more of a healthy look than a burned one. Groomed and rested looking, he was quite handsome, and it was apparent he had the look of success all over him. Mrs. Diamond did not look like the Mrs. Diamond they had plucked from the ocean the day before. She was radiant, beautifully groomed, a lady of distinction and class, yet able to fit in around the boating crowd, not afraid to tie off a line, tie on a scuba tank and go for a hundred foot underwater adventure, and not too good to take turns at the cleaning table when the catch was good.

Gaffer tossed the first line over and Jeremy pulled the boat a little to port to line it up in the slip, and then he tied off to an iron dock cleat. When the second line was tossed over, Jessica caught it, and in a single motion wrapped the cleat and locked it down. Max secured a spring line while Gaffer and P.J. took care of the bow lines. Max handed the electrical shore power cord across to Jeremy who knew exactly what to do with it. A minute later Billy turned the engines off. The silence was wonderful. One-by-one the passengers jumped onto the dock and were greeted with handshakes and hugs from Mr. and Mrs. Diamond. Jessica produced two very large shopping bags filled with the crews clothes, all cleaned and folded. Max was as glad to see his good windbreaker, as Gaffer was his Bimini Twist tee shirt.

It was just turning noon when they docked. There was plenty of time left in the day to clean up the boat and the fishing gear. Jeremy Diamond insisted, rather begged the *Fearless Flyer* crew and passengers to let him buy them lunch at the yacht club restaurant. Everyone accepted, and they headed up the dock to the club house.

In spite of what appeared to be a great deal of wealth and breeding, the Diamonds were a very down to earth couple. They could talk about the down and dirty of boat maintenance, they knew fishing, scuba diving, and offshore power boat racing. They were aware of the problems and frustrations of sea captains and their mates. There **was no** pretense at all, and they never failed to mention how much they **owed** to the present company for having rescued them.

The luncheon took an hour, and Gaffer was beginning to become anxious. The salt was drying on *Fearless Flyer* and he wanted to attack it before it became a permanent part of the stainless steel, glass, and paint. He excused himself from the table and headed down to the boat. He could not wait to get some fresh water on it.

Jeremy Diamond said that he had already discussed his claim with the insurance company. He said the adjuster acted like this sort of thing happens everyday and took the report and would process it. He would be calling on all of the people on board *Fearless Flyer* and *Jump-In* for statements, and then would pay the claim.

"Will you order a new boat?" asked Max.

"We'll get a new boat," said Jeremy. "I don't think we'll build one this time. It takes over a year, and it also takes a lot of time and energy. Jessica and I have been discussing going to some yacht brokers and boat shows. It might suit us better to buy something that's fairly new and immediately available."

"Did you have anything in mind?" asked Billy.

Jeremy shook his head. "We only lost our boat yesterday. Until then we were all set." He added, "But, I have an idea or two."

Jessica's eyes flooded and tears began to fall down her cheeks. "We loved that boat," she sobbed. Everyone at the table shifted uncomfortably. She took a moment to compose herself and added, "We built that boat together. It had so many of our memories on it, family pictures, a small library of our favorite nautical books, some clothing that wasn't worth anything, but that meant a lot to us. You know, like a souvenir tee shirt from a great vacation in Key West, or a special Guy Harvey jacket signed by the artist. Little things. But things that carry a lot of sentiment. While I couldn't be more appreciative to be alive **and to** have my husband and brother safe, my heart is truly broken **when I** think about what went down with that boat."

"I completely understand that," said Max. "I sympathize with you. It must be just awful."

"Awful," repeated Jessica through tears.

"To answer your question, Captain Billy," said Jeremy, "I think I'll look at something smaller and less maintenance for my next boat. I really don't like being a gentleman yachtsman. I'm more of a hands-on kind of person. I might get something in the fifty foot or less class that I can run myself with my wife, and perhaps a mate instead of a captain. I have owned several boats and I know pretty much about operating them."

Looking out over the yacht basin Billy pointed down to *Fearless Flyer.* "You see that boy right there?" he asked, pointing at Gaffer who was standing on the bridge with a fresh water hose washing down everything in sight that could possibly have salt on it. "That boy is the best mate in South Florida. I've worked with a bunch of them but there's no one like Gaffer. He loves to fish, he loves boats, and he's willing to work hard until the job is done."

Max beamed with pride. "Thank you , Billy. It pleases me to hear you say that."

"Oh," said Jessica, "Is that your son? I didn't get that."

"And so is he," said Max nodding toward P.J.

"Oh. You're so fortunate, two beautiful boys. How very nice," said Jessica.

"Thank you," said Max.

"So, are you a family of captains and mates?" asked Jeremy.

Max laughed, but not meaning to make Jeremy feel foolish he explained, "We are friends of Captain Billy. He hired Gaffer to mate for him in the tournament, and invited us to come spend the week with them. We're just along for the fun of it and to help out."

"Some fun," said P.J. sarcastically.

Max leaned over toward Jessica, "P.J. doesn't share our love of boating, fishing, or Bimini."

"Yes," said Ashley primly, "Like me, P.J. gets seasick." P.J.'s face flushed as everyone at the table chuckled.

"So, I should keep Gaffer's phone number handy when I'm looking for a mate," said Jeremy.

"You'd be doing yourself a big favor," said Billy.

Jeremy took his wallet from his back pocket and handed it to Jessica. "Will you take care of this?" He was referring to the check for lunch. He slid his chair back and stood. "Excuse me, I need to have a word with my new first mate." He left the restaurant and headed down the dock to where Gaffer was busy with a bucket of soapy water and a long handled brush. He climbed the ladder to the bridge and leaned against the captain's chair. "Billy tells me you're the best first mate around," he said.

Gaffer smiled. "Billy said that?"

"Said you were the best mate in all of South Florida?"

"He said that?"

"He did," said Jeremy.

"He never told me that," said Gaffer. "He must worry that I'll ask him for a raise." Gaffer was smiling and joking.

"Could be," agreed Jeremy. "But that's what I want to talk to you about. You know, mating for me."

Gaffer looked confused. "Did you forget that you don't **have a** boat anymore?"

"How could I forget that?" remarked Jeremy. "But soon enough I'll get another one, and I'll be looking for a mate."

"I'm always looking for mating jobs," said Gaffer. "But I **don't** know." He hesitated for a moment. "You're kind of like a yachtsman. I'm really only looking for fishing gigs."

"That's perfect. I mostly want to fish. I'm not really a yachter. *Dream Machine* was a mistake. A big Garlington like that, all fancy. I had a love/hate relationship with that boat. I loved it because it **was so** beautiful and so well made. There was never anything to complain about, for sure. But on the other hand, it took days to get ready to go cruising. It was too big for my taste, and way too much mainten**ance.**"

After a brief pause Jeremy added, "I want to get something I can **handle** myself without a whole crew. I just want one person to mate for me and who knows his way around fishing. Captain Billy says you're that person."

Gaffer considered. This was beginning to sound very good. "We could talk. I like it simple and informal. I won't wear a uniform or serve cocktails, but I will tie knots and rig baits."

Jeremy laughed. "And I'll make you an offer you simply can't refuse."

Now Gaffer laughed. "Tough guy, huh?"

Then they both laughed together. Jeremy knew he liked this boy and wanted him to work on his boat. Gaffer was thinking they might have a lot in common. "What kind of boat did you have in mind?"

"To me, the most beautiful boat, the most perfect fishing machine, is the fifty foot Open Viking."

Gaffer's mouth dropped open. He could only gape.

"I see I've touched a nerve," said Jeremy.

"We have identical taste," said Gaffer. "I have loved that boat since the first day I laid eyes on it. I'd work on that one for free."

"Not a chance," said Jeremy. "I'll pay you well for honest work. I'll insist on it."

Gaffer was shocked. He could say nothing. It took **several** seconds before he could compose himself enough to speak. "**Mr.** Diamond, am I dreaming or am I being offered a job working for you on a Viking Fifty?"

Jeremy Diamond had been listening carefully to Gaffer **and** taking in his speech and mannerisms. He knew right away that **Gaffer's** qualities ran deep and that he would be an asset on a fishing trip, **or just** to help around the boat.

"You're not dreaming," said Jeremy. "In fact I not only want you to say that you'll work on my boat, but I also want you to help me find the boat, buy the boat, and provision the boat. Every bit of fishing **gear** I owned went down on *Dream Machine*. I don't have so much as **a bait** rod."

In his naivete Gaffer offered, "It's OK, Mr. Diamond. I can lend you some stuff until you get outfitted. I can tell you exactly **what to** buy."

"I would appreciate your help very much. But first, I have an important rule for you to follow if you're going to work for me."

"What?"

"You have to call me Jeremy. We're going to cruise together, fish together, and live together when we're on the boat. You have to get used to calling me Jeremy and my wife Jessica. I have plenty of people who work for me who call me Mr. Diamond. It's not what I want to hear when I'm relaxing on my boat."

Gaffer shrugged. "No problem, Jeremy. Whatever you say."

"So, you'll take the job?" asked Jeremy.

"I want to be certain that you understand my limitations," said Gaffer. "I'm still in school, and that comes first. I also have to make a bunch of trips with my dad to Bimini each summer. That's a priority."

"We'll work around our schedules. I work too and have a family to tend to. I cruise and fish when I can. When we can work **it out** together, we'll do it. I can always call Jimmy Pile if you're not **available.**

81

But, I'll always call you first. I want you on my first team. If we can understand that, we can have a deal."

Gaffer extended his hand to Jeremy Diamond. "You have a new first mate," he said.

Jeremy accepted the handshake and met Gaffer eye to eye. "I could not be more delighted. Something great came of this otherwise miserable weekend." Jeremy hesitated for a moment and considered. "You didn't ask about the pay. Aren't you curious?"

Gaffer shrugged. "I'm sure you'll pay me what's fair. You'll grow to appreciate me on board and find suitable compensation."

"Yes, I will," said Jeremy. Then he added, "The big boat show is in Fort Lauderdale next week. How about you and me and Jessica go down there and see if there's anything we like."

"Can I bring my dad? We usually go to the boat show together."

"Rule number two," said Jeremy. "Whenever you go with us, your dad, your brother and anybody else in your family is invited. Sometimes you can bring a friend. But always Max and P.J. are welcome."

"You don't have to do that. My dad is good on a boat, but my brother is useless. Why don't we take it as it comes."

"OK, we'll take it as it comes. Just so you know it's all good."

"It's all good," said Gaffer.

Max walked down the dock in deep conversation with Billy while P.J., Jessica, and Ashley walked behind them and talked about how they were going to complete Ashley's arrangements for the trip home to Denver. Jessica offered to help and started by dialing 800 information for the airline's telephone number. She was a resourceful person and within ten minutes had made arrangements for an evening flight out of Miami through Dallas and into Denver in the middle of the night.

There was a big friendly good bye when Jeremy, Jessica and Ashley left. More telephone numbers were exchanged, handshakes, **hugs**, and P.J. received the kiss from Ashley he had been hoping for.

As the Diamonds walked away with Ashley in tow, Gaffer turned to his father. "Mr. Diamond wants me to work on his new boat when he gets it."

"I heard Billy put in a good word for you. Don't forget to **thank** him."

Gaffer turned to Billy. "What did you say?"

"He said he was going to get a smaller boat and all he would need would be a mate. I just told him that he'd be doing himself a big favor by talking to you about the job."

"Well, I need to thank you then 'cause I definitely got the job. He wants me to go with him to help pick out a new boat at the boat show in Fort Lauderdale next week. Then he wants me to help him buy all the fishing gear for it. He lost all his when the Garlington went down."

Max chuckled. "You've landed the job of your dreams. Good for you."

"He also said you are invited on any trips we take, you and P.J., any family members, and sometimes I can take a friend."

"Sounds good for you," said Max. "You might be all set."

"I told him about not being permanently available because I'm in school and that we need time to take our own trips. He said 'cool' and that we could work around it. When I'm not available he'll call Jimmy Pile."

"What a deal," said Max. "It sort of answers your questions about a summer job."

A line of concern appeared to cross Gaffer's face. "He's being so nice. Do you think it's for real?"

"Do you have a doubt?" asked Max.

"Only in that it seems too good to be true."

"I know it's like a dream or something, but I wouldn't be too suspicious. The Diamonds seem genuinely nice to me. From just talking over lunch I can tell that Jessica is a real lady, no pretense. Jeremy seems genuine to me. Think about it, we truly saved their lives yesterday. They have a lot to be thankful for. And they didn't have to come here today to see us and bring our clothes all cleaned and everything. That was a genuinely nice gesture. I feel like they can be trusted."

"Man," said Gaffer, "it all seems so good."

"Sometimes good things happen to good people. Today it's your turn. Enjoy it."

EIGHT

Lady Liberty

Jeremy Diamond kept his word and invited Gaffer and Max to meet him at the main pavilion of the Broward County Convention Center on the Wednesday before the boat show opened. He had four VIP passes, one each for himself, his wife, Gaffer, and Max. He and Jessica were standing just outside the main entrance waiting for the Carsons to arrive. As soon as they met up, the foursome was whisked away in a private shuttle to be taken to the in-water displays at Marina del Mar. The shuttle, which was provided by Exclusive Yacht Brokers for seriously interested shoppers, deposited the group at its main sales center which, for purposes of this show, was a seventy two meter Bennetti manufactured in Viareggio, Italy.

'Crazy' Sam Trumble was assigned to be their account representative. Crazy Sam had worked with the Diamonds on the purchase and construction of *Dream Machine* and they knew they could work with him, and more importantly, they trusted him. There was nothing crazy about Crazy Sam. He was sharp, honest, hard working and had three decades of experience in yachting and yacht brokerage. He was the perfect man for what the Diamonds were looking for.

Prior to scheduling this appointment, Jeremy Diamond had told Crazy Sam the type of boat that would interest him. Sam had several for him to look at. Not all were Vikings; there was a Luhrs that Sam wanted him to see, and a Predator that he thought might be the right kind of deal for him. Additionally there were two Vikings in the configuration that Jeremy had asked for. Max and Gaffer followed the parade in and out of the Luhrs and the Predator, but they never really found anything to get excited about. In Gaffer's description, the Luhrs was nice, but not in the same class as the Viking. The Predator was nice too, and it was the right configuration, but it was about half the size of the boat the Diamonds were looking for. Gaffer expressed this to Jeremy who agreed whole-heartedly.

"Please, Sam. Don't waste any more of our time," said Jeremy. "I have asked these friends to accompany me here today to do some serious looking. If you can't show me the Viking I'm looking for, please say so and let me get on with my search."

"Hold on," said Sam. "I have two Vikings for you to see. I just wanted to let you know about these others because they are in special circumstances and you might be able to make a deal that would have you see them a little differently."

"Look, Sam. I'm not an idiot. So they're bank repos. Who cares? I said Open Viking and that's all I have time for today."

"No problem," said Sam. "I'm sorry to have wasted your time, and of course your guests' time. I have your Vikings right this way."

They walked for fifteen minutes along first the concrete piers, and then along the floating docks. The area was a beehive of activity. Workmen were moving floating sections around, pilots were parking some of the largest, most expensive yachts in the world, and about two thousand visitors had the same kind of VIP passes that the Diamonds and

Carsons were carrying. But that number was nothing compared to the twenty thousand people who would mob the show each of the next five days. They passed literally hundreds of boats for sale by owner, Hatteras, Bertrams, Buddy Davis, Post, all the big names. They passed a single Open Viking that Gaffer stuck in his memory to check out later. It was older and poorly maintained, but it had possibilities.

Finally Crazy Sam led them up to the Viking exhibit. Jeremy found it interesting. Viking was branching out into much fancier, modern designs. The boats kept getting bigger and pricier. But the sports models were well made, intelligently designed fishing machines. The foursome crawled all over the two boats, onto the bridge, into the cabins, galley, engine rooms, every possible storage space, including ice chests, live bait well, and fish boxes. They examined controls, electronics, sleeping space, as well as specifications for water and fuel storage, cruising capabilities and communications. This truly was the perfect boat.

While Jeremy and Max sat with the Viking representative to go over pricing and delivery, Gaffer and Jessica wandered down the dock to satisfy their love of gawking at boats. They were two blocks away from the Viking exhibit when Gaffer heard his name called. He turned to see who was calling him but saw nobody he recognized. He heard his name again and looked around. Oh, there! His friend from back in middle school, the young boy who had first introduced him to fishing, Jason Court. They hadn't seen each other in two years.

Jessica followed Gaffer over to meet young Jason, who was standing on the transom of a forty-three foot Phoenix and facing the dock. Gaffer introduced them and greetings were exchanged.

"Is this your boat?" asked Gaffer.

"It's our family boat," said Jason. "My dad wants to sell it so we can get a bigger boat. He wants that fifty-five Hatt with the tower over on Pier J."

"Sweet," said Gaffer. "Any takers for this one?"

"It's too early in the show to tell. A few different people asked to come on board. My dad calls them tire kickers. They walked around and looked at everything. Asked some questions. We gave out our phone numbers a few times. It's not easy," said Jason.

"Boats are moving slow?" asked Jessica.

"I've heard a few complaints from my dad and some of the other men. I think it's slow. They're calling it a buyers' market."

"Do you know what that means?" asked Jessica.

"Best I can figure is everybody's trying to sell boats and not enough people are trying to buy boats." Jason looked puzzled. "Is that right."

Jessica smiled at the boy. "That's exactly right."

Jason turned back to Gaffer. "Are you and your dad buying a new boat? I thought you loved *Bimini Twist.*"

"No, no," said Gaffer. "We're good with *Bimini Twist.* We're here to help Mrs. Diamond and her husband find a boat. They're looking for a Viking Open Fifty."

"I saw one," said Jason. "There's one for sale."

"There's two over at the Viking dealer," said Gaffer.

Jason was animated. "No, man. I mean there's a really sweet one that's for sale by the owner, not a broker or the dealer. You need to see this boat."

Gaffer and Jessica were both interested. "Where is it?" asked Jessica. "Does it have a tower?"

"Huge tower," said Jason. "Let's see." He had lost his sense of direction. He looked around and then pointed across the basin. "You have to go down here to the third left turn and then look to the right."

"Come with us," said Gaffer.

"Can't. I have to stay here until my dad gets back. Call me later."

"OK, I'll call you. Thanks for the lead on the boat."

Gaffer and Jessica walked off to find their Viking. They tried one left turn, then another, and then another. They were lost and turned around amid hundreds of yachts, but eventually they made the correct turn and came across the boat they were looking for. Considering that the boat show had not yet opened, there were a disturbing number of people interested in it. Three different parties were climbing all over it, checking out the bunks, the galley, the electronics. There was even a father son team on the top of the tower. Undaunted Gaffer and Jessica climbed aboard. They found the owner and spent a few minutes going over the features of the boat and inquiring about the asking price. $875,000 seemed reasonable compared to what a new one would cost. This one was only one year old and had only eighty hours on the engines. It was as good as new, perhaps better.

"How firm are you on that price?" asked Jessica. "Before you answer, let me say that my husband and I have a better than even chance of walking out of here today with a new boat, and this is very close to what we are looking for."

"I have some flexibility," said the owner. "Why don't you go find your husband and I'll put on a pot of coffee."

"Do that," said Jessica. "We'll be back as soon as possible. Give me, say a half hour."

"You've got it."

"I'll stay here," said Gaffer. "I want to learn the boat."

Jessica hurried down the dock to find the Viking display where she had left her husband and Max. When she arrived fifteen minutes later, she found Jeremy closely examining the fine print of a purchase agreement. He was just waiting for her to return so he could get her blessing on the purchase. The new boat would have to be built. It would take eight months and cost $977,000. The tower would cost an additional $60,000 and take two more months to build and install. Jessica took her husband aside out of earshot of Crazy Sam and the dealer. Max joined them.

"We found what we're looking for in a nearly new boat. It's only got a few hours on the engines, it's cleaner than new, and a lot less expensive."

"I'm listening," said Jeremy. "How did you find it?"

"Gaffer ran into a friend who knew about it."

Max looked around. He frowned, "Where is Gaffer?"

"He stayed on the boat. By the time we get there he'll have the entire lowdown on every part of it."

Max nodded. "We better get over there before there's no chance of saying no. If you don't buy it, I'll have to."

Jeremy and Jessica laughed. They knew he was right.

Three hours later the Carsons and the Diamonds left the show, smiles all around, highly animated and in somewhat disbelief of their success this day. Jeremy and Jessica Diamond were going to be the new owners of that fifty foot Viking. This was Wednesday. The boat would be locked in the marina until the show broke down. Their surveyor would come during the weekend to examine every square inch of the boat and its systems. On Tuesday, when the portable docks were taken down and the Viking was released from its imprisonment in the marina, they would have a sea trial. That trial was scheduled for 3:30 in the afternoon so Gaffer could have time to get out of school and shoot down to Fort Lauderdale in time for the ride. From the sea trial they would return to the dock for the formal signing of the transfer and title papers.

The name, *Lady Liberty*, sounded right and they decided to keep it. Jeremy credited Gaffer with helping him to save a year of waiting and nearly $200,000. In his excitement for the new boat, Jeremy promised to buy the best tender a fisherman could ever dream of, and the newest and best fishing gear available.

Max agreed that Gaffer could skip school on Wednesday to help deliver the boat to its new home behind the Diamond residence on the Gables Waterway. Jeremy promised Gaffer that he would let him drive the boat all the way there, forty miles away. As Jeremy put it, "Gaffer, you're going to have to know everything about this boat, including how to drive it, dock it, and take care of it. You might as well start now."

The smile on Gaffer's face masked the pounding in his heart. Mr. Diamond was going to keep his word and make Gaffer his truly valuable first mate. Gaffer would get the kind of time on the bridge that would qualify him for his captain's license. This was almost too good to be true.

Gaffer might just as well not gone to school on Tuesday. His mind was on *Lady Liberty* and he spent the entire day watching the clock. He couldn't remember a time when it moved slower than this day. But eventually, agonizingly slowly, the second hand on the clock on the wall swept by the twelve and a loud bell rang. The teacher was saying something but Gaffer did not hear it. He darted for the door, out into the parking lot and into his car. He was the first student out of the school, and five minutes later was entering I 95 southbound for Fort Lauderdale. He took out his cell phone and dialed the number Jessica Diamond had given him. Her caller ID displayed the name and number of Gaffer Carson. She picked up on the second ring.

"Hello, Gaffer. Are you on your way?"

"Hi, Jessica. I'm on I 95, about thirty minutes from the marina."

"OK. We're on the boat now with the surveyor. So far things look good. No problems."

"Great," said Gaffer. "I'll be there as soon as I can."

"Gaffer," said Jessica. "Please don't hurry. We'll wait. I don't want you driving dangerously. It's not that important."

Gaffer slowed back down to seventy. "OK, Jessica. I just slowed down. I'll be careful."

"Good. We'll see you when you get here. Drive safely."

They rang off and Gaffer concentrated on his driving. This was no time to drive foolishly. He had important business to attend to and he didn't want to make any mistakes that would slow him down.

"C'mon Gaffer," Jessica Diamond called down the dock when she saw him coming a hundred and fifty feet away. Gaffer could see the diesel exhaust fumes coming from the back of the boat and he broke into a run. By the time he was standing on the dock next to the boat, all of the lines had been cast off and the owner was at the helm showing Jeremy and the surveyor some of the controls with which they were not familiar. All three greeted Gaffer and shook his hand as he joined them for the introduction to the controls. They knew that they might not get another opportunity to find out first hand how each dial, gauge, lever, and switch worked. Jeremy took notes in an important looking planner, Jessica took her notes on an electronic Palm Pilot. Gaffer watched and listened and asked questions incessantly.

With the dock lines released there was no time to sit idly by waiting for the wind or current to push *Lady Liberty* against a piling. The owner eased her out of the slip and used starboard reverse and forward port to turn the boat to the right. It obeyed perfectly and in a few seconds was sitting at a ninety degree angle to its position when it left the slip. The owner stepped aside and handed control to Jeremy. But true to his word, he deferred to Gaffer who now stood at the helm ready to slip the gears into forward. At idle speed he eased out of the marina and into the waterway. He used the opposite maneuver, port reverse and starboard forward to make the boat turn sharply to the left. It handled like a powerful and obedient, well-trained athlete. For a boat dozens of times larger than *Bimini Twist*, the boat that Gaffer was used to maneuvering, this boat was every bit as easy to control.

Out in the open Intercoastal there was nothing to do but watch for traffic and poke along slow enough to not throw a wake. The owner, the surveyor, and Jeremy, disappeared below so they could have a tour of the engine room. They had intakes, exhausts, pumps, switches, meters, valves, and instruments to check out. That left Gaffer alone at the wheel while Jessica made herself comfortable on the sofa along side the helm. Gaffer had the whole show to himself. He was not expecting that. One minute he was surrounded by people who knew exactly how to handle this magnificent machine, the next he was there doing it all himself.

His first test came when he approached the Seventeenth Street Bridge. He didn't know whether to hold for an opening or continue under it. He looked up at the tower that appeared at that moment to be about 300 feet high, when in fact it was more like thirty five feet tall. He chose to err on the side of caution and ask for an opening. He tuned the VHS to channel nine and keyed the mike.

"Seventeenth Street Bridge, this is *Lady Liberty* requesting an opening on the quarter hour, over."

Gaffer could not see it but the bridge tender was carefully eyeing the boat. The radio crackled back. "*Lady Liberty*, this is Seventeenth Street Bridge. Are you certain you need an opening?"

Gaffer was honest with the bridge tender. "Seventeenth Street Bridge, this is *Lady Liberty*. I'm not entirely certain, but I've never driven this boat under this bridge, and I don't know how much clearance I have. Over."

"Ten-four, *Lady Liberty*. I'll give you an opening on the quarter hour."

"Ten-four, *Lady Liberty* out."

Now for the first time Gaffer was visibly nervous. He was at the helm in complete control. The boat had to stand still and wait for the opening, and there was a knot and a half current trying to force him into the bridge. Gaffer looked around quickly to get a fix on what was going on around him. He was thankful that it was a weekday and there was practically no traffic. But he could definitely feel the current moving the boat, and he had to do something about that before it resulted in an accident. Again he looked around and saw that he was clear to move about anywhere he wanted. He used the same logic to maneuver *Lady Liberty* that he would to maneuver *Bimini Twist.* At idle speed he placed both engines in reverse. He gave a little extra gas to the starboard engine and the boat started to swing into the middle of the channel and away from the bridge. He backed up 200 feet and lined up with the center of the span. He shifted into forward with both engines to take the weigh off the boat. In less than five seconds the boat stopped moving and sat directly in the middle of the waterway looking straight at the center of the bridge span. It was a good maneuver. Gaffer was not wearing a watch, so he would not know when the quarter hour would arrive, but he was comfortable with his distance from the bridge and was hopeful that there would be no more maneuvering before the span opened.

The examination below was going well. The three men were engrossed in a discussion of blocked cooling lines, and gave no thought to the fact that a sixteen year old boy had the responsibility to keep the boat safe from damage. They felt the boat stop, and they felt it go into reverse as it moved away from the bridge. No one was at all concerned.

At last the loud bell on the bridge sounded. Gaffer watched as the traffic control arms came down, stopping anyone from entering the span. Red lights flashed, the bell rang, and traffic came to a standstill. A moment later the bridge sections began to rise. Gaffer waited patently until both bridge sections were completely upright. He then placed both engines into forward and idled up to the bridge and then through the opening. He took it directly in the center of the span. He held his breath, and a minute later it was over. The bridge was behind him. He gave two hits on the horn as a courtesy to the bridge tender, and continued south for 300 yards. A wave of relief washed over him. Jessica Diamond could see it but said nothing. She knew this was new territory for Gaffer, not in the sense that he had never driven through this spot before, he was well familiar with the Intercoastal in Fort Lauderdale, and he knew his way around Port Everglades. What she sensed was that Gaffer had just made a maneuver with a large yacht that was like none other he had tried before. She said nothing, but allowed him the moment.

The Port Everglades inlet was upon them. Gaffer turned to Jessica. "I'm assuming that we are going outside. Is that your understanding."

"It is," replied Jessica. "But that's an assumption. I'll go ask." She made her way down the four stairs to where her husband was talking with the seller of the boat and the surveyor. He stopped talking to hear what she wanted. "Did you mean to run outside?" she asked.

"Definitely," said Jeremy. "Out the inlet and then east and north."

Jessica turned and rejoined Gaffer at the helm. "Outside," she said.

"Aye, aye," said Gaffer. He never said that. He wondered what made him say it. Then he understood. His nervousness had completely left him and he was feeling good about himself and about the position he was in. He was happy and clear headed. He felt invincible.

NINE

Maiden Voyage

Gaffer used his cell phone to call home. His mother picked up as soon as she saw on the caller ID that it was her son. "So, how was it?" asked Lisa Carson.

"Let's just say it passed the test. Mr. Diamond is signing the papers right now. It's really happening. He's going to own this boat in about an hour."

"Then congratulations. What do you think?"

"What do you mean?"

"I mean about the boat. How do you like it?"

"I'm not sure. I might be in shock. I've never experienced anything quite like it."

Lisa laughed. She knew it would be so.

"Mom, I'm not going to school tomorrow. Can I spend the night on the boat?"

"Who said you're not going to school tomorrow?"

"Dad said it was OK."

"Nobody told me," Lisa said with concern in her voice.

"Dad said I could. I thought he cleared it with you."

"It's OK, I just didn't know."

"So can I stay here over night. We're going to deliver the boat to the Diamond's house in the morning."

"OK, you might as well." Lisa and Gaffer spoke for another couple of minutes before ringing off. Gaffer relayed the good news to Jeremy. It was now well past sundown and a quarter moon and nearby street light were all that lit the marina. The previous owner had gone home with his closing papers and a check in the amount of $840,000. Gaffer could see that the man was saddened at having to sell his treasured yacht. It had been obvious that he loved it, he had taken exquisite care of it. The past two hours had been taken up with a private tour of the boat, given to Gaffer by the man who was now the previous owner. Gaffer had his own notebook, taking notes, writing down all the preferred gauge settings, where to take on fuel, water, what parts needed oil, grease, soap, polish, paint, and so forth. By the time the tour was complete, Gaffer had five pages of notes and his head was swimming.

Finally, at a few minutes before midnight, the Diamonds climbed onto the dock and said goodnight to Gaffer. Jeremy drove in his car while Jessica followed him in Gaffer's car. The Diamonds planned on rising early the following morning and driving back to Fort Lauderdale for the deadhead trip with the boat to its new berth behind their house in Coral Gables. Then Gaffer was to take one of them back up to Fort Lauderdale to pick up their car.

Alone with the responsibility for the entire boat, Gaffer thought he would be too excited to sleep. He found out otherwise when the Diamonds left. He toured the outside of the boat one more time, checking dock lines and fenders. The boat sat at peace in its slip, the docks were empty of traffic, everything was well under control.

Gaffer moved into the small living room and turned on the television set. By the time he found a program that interested him and sat down to relax, he was nearly too tired to keep his eyes open. After he found himself dozing off for the second time he turned the television off and climbed into his bunk. He was asleep a minute later.

The clock on the wall told Gaffer it was 6:00 AM when his eyes first opened. He looked around at his surroundings and placed his hand on the bulkhead next to him. It was hard to believe that he was not dreaming. He rose slowly and made his way into the bathroom. The first order of business was to grab a shower to wake himself up. The bathroom had everything he needed to make himself ready for the day. He found a clean *Lady Liberty* tee shirt and put it on. He opened the cabin door to let in the fresh morning air and to check dock lines and the general condition of things. It was all as it should be so he went back inside and made himself some breakfast.

When Gaffer turned on his cell phone he was surprised to find that he had already missed a call from Jeremy Diamond. He immediately hit the redial button and waited for Mr. Diamond to answer. It took only two rings before they were connected.

"Good morning, Gaffer. How's our new toy?"

"Our new toy," thought Gaffer. Some toy. "Perfect," he answered. "I've already been outside checking everything. It rode out the night perfectly. I'll be ready to go whenever you get here."

"I'm glad to hear that everything is good. I appreciate your staying on board last night. It gave me comfort knowing that you were there."

"I didn't know how whipped I was last night. I was in bed a half hour after you left. But I'm good now. That bunk is excellent."

"I'm glad to her that," replied Jeremy. "Listen, Gaffer, there's been a change of plans. I can't get back up there today. Jessica and I have something we must do. We can't get out of it. We were looking forward to the trip as much as you."

"Oh," said Gaffer. The disappointment in his voice was evident. He thought about the consequences of that statement and realized he was stranded with his car forty miles away in Coral Gables. "You have my car, what should we do?"

Jeremy answered cautiously. "My wife and I discussed it, and we think the best thing would be if you could bring the boat on down here. Do you think you could manage that?"

Gaffer's heart leapt into his throat. That was a lot of responsibility. His voice was shaky. "You mean me bring the boat to your house alone?"

"Unless you can find someone to come with you. You can bring a friend if you like, it's up to you."

Gaffer thought about it for several seconds. This would be a test of his skill and courage, a test like he had been looking forward to forever. He brought the strength back into his voice. "No problem," he said. "I can be there before noon. When will you be home?"

"Jessica and I have been called out of town. We won't be here until late tonight. We'll leave your car keys with the housekeeper."

"Fine then," said Gaffer. "I'll deliver the boat and clean it up when I get to your dock. You'll have your brand new shiny boat waiting for you when you get home tonight."

"Thank you so much Gaffer. I'm sorry we had to do this, but this came up at the last minute. I have confidence that you'll be fine getting down here." Jeremy gave directions to his house from the mouth of the Coral Gables waterway. "When you reach the first channel marker, call my house. The housekeeper will come down to the dock and catch the lines for you." Gaffer acknowledged, accepted a few more instructions, and they hung up. Gaffer then got busy looking for charts.

He looked high and low for a chart desk or cabinet. After ten frustrating minutes he remembered that the charts were in the GPS. He dialed up the Port Everglades to Elliott Key chart and zoomed in on the area from Government Cut to Fowey Rocks. The eleven inch display gave every possible landmark in vivid detail. Gaffer examined it for a minute and was soon convinced that he had everything he needed to find his way safely. He had only navigated on Biscayne Bay a few times, and did not know the channels that well.

One thing that was a priority was that Gaffer wanted to avoid bridges. He would have to navigate the Seventeenth Street Bridge one more time, and after that he could stay outside. It looked to him like the entrance through Stiltsville would be the best route into Biscayne Bay. He knew it was a narrow, winding channel, but well marked. After that, it would be a straight shot to the waterway. He viewed the speed dial on his cell phone and called his father.

"Dad, the Diamonds can't get back to go with me to take the boat home. They asked me to do it. You want to go?"

"Sorry, Gaff, not today. I'm slammed." There did not seem to be any concern in Max's voice as to Gaffer's ability to deliver the boat. He didn't even ask how Gaffer felt about it. This gave Gaffer that much more confidence.

Sooner or later he would have to become comfortable with this type of responsibility. This was as good a time as any. He said good bye to his father and promised to call when the boat was docked at the Diamond's house. He sat quietly for several minutes thinking about how he should plan this short trip. First of all there was the dock lines, shore power and utilities, water, cable and telephone. All those things had to be stowed carefully before the trip began. No, first start the engines so he could be ready to go as soon as he was untied. No, first the generator because the shore power was going to be disconnected. Yeah, that seemed right. Gaffer's head was swimming. All these little things to remember, any one of which he could mess up and would make him look bad. Now he got it, first check the weather. If the seas were any higher than three to five feet, he would go down by the Intercoastal Waterway. It would take a couple of hours longer and he would have dozens of bridges, but perhaps a slow idle down to Miami would not be so bad.

Gaffer's head was spinning. Too many thoughts coming at him at once. First check the weather. That was first. He went out to the bridge and tuned the VHS radio to the weather channel. The familiar voice was giving reports for Okeechobee and other area to the north and west of Fort Lauderdale, but that was all right. His first clue would come from the wind speed and it didn't matter whether that was from his present location or another area of Florida. He listened. "Wind out of the southwest at ten knots." So far, very good. Ten knots was nothing. Southwest wind meant if he stayed within a mile of the coast, the land would block the wind from kicking up the seas near shore. He listened further and the report started giving sea conditions starting at Stuart and moving down the coast. It seemed that everywhere near shore the wind was light and the seas were nearly negligible. Then finally it came, the weather from Jupiter Inlet to Key Largo and out fifty miles. Same thing, south to southwest wind, five to ten knots, small gusts to fifteen. Seas three feet or less. That was it. He was definitely going outside.

Gaffer made a quick tour of the cabin to make certain everything that could be secured, was. Then that was it. He walked out onto the deck and closed the door behind him. The first thing on his mental checklist was to start the engines. He did that, no problem. Next, start the generator. Simple, hit the button and listen for it to start. It did. OK, so a big hurdle had been passed. The engines and generator were started. Next, disconnect the shore power and bring the heavy shore power cord on board and store it. Five minutes later that was done. He hated the shore power cord, it was very heavy and hard to coil. He was happy to drop it into the lazarette and close the compartment door. He then disconnected the TV cable and phone. He wound the narrow cords and placed them inside the cabin on the floor out of the way. He would be using that again as soon as he docked. The water hose had already been stored but it made him think. He checked the fresh water gauge on his dashboard. It read two thirds full. That was about two hundred gallons. More than he could need in a week. He turned on the depth finder and radar. He called for a radio check and immediately heard a response from a boat two miles offshore indicating that his signal was loud and clear. He thanked the sailor and hung up the handset.

Next Gaffer would have to work fairly fast. The fenders had to come off and he would have to be ready to pull out of the slip very soon after that. Not that the wind was pushing the boat around, just that he was uncomfortable with the whole idea of being in the slip without his fenders out. It made him feel naked. Speaking of naked, Gaffer stopped for a minute. Did he have to go to the bathroom before he left. This would be his last chance. No, he was OK. He climbed onto the dock and untied both stern lines. He did not need them before he took down the fenders. Those fenders were making him nuts. Now the stern lines were on board. The fenders on the starboard side were doing nothing anyhow, there was no dock or boat on that side. He brought them in. Next, the bow lines. Loosen them up and slip them off the pilings. That too was much easier than he had dreaded. Gaffer knew he was thinking much too fast for his own good. He took a couple of deep cleansing breaths to relax and immediately took in the port side fenders. A single spring line was all that was left, and he would be ready to go. The boat had still failed to move in its slip. It was behaving very nicely. He walked around to where the spring line was tied to a cleat on the dock. He unwrapped it and then loosened it from the spring cleat on the deck. He had five dock lines sitting in an array all over the cockpit. It was not the way he liked to keep things ship shape, normally he would coil them up neatly and store them. But, since *Lady Liberty* was sitting in the slip with nothing keeping it from moving in a current or breeze, he was more concentrated on making certain he was in control. The dock lines could wait.

Gaffer's heart was in his throat. He was at the helm of this incredible machine, being trusted by its owner to deliver it safely to its new home in Coral Gables. His heart was pounding and hands were shaking. A new sense of urgency overcame him. He had nothing to do but what he had trained himself to do most of his life. He shifted the controls forward and then back into neutral. *Lady Liberty* eased out of its slip and floated into the marina turning basin. There was no time to worry now, the boat was under weigh. Gaffer gave it starboard reverse and port forward. It turned to the right and lined up with the mouth of the basin. Gaffer took the starboard control and placed it into forward. The boat moved smoothly forward. He went back to neutral with both controls. The boat drifted out into the Intercoastal. He needed a left turn to get the correct heading. Port reverse and starboard forward, all at idle speed. A perfect left turn. Gaffer simply moved the port control to the forward position and he was headed straight down the Intercoastal toward the Seventeenth Street Bridge. Ahead he saw good news. A mega sailboat from the boat show named *Sargasso* was waiting a half mile ahead for the bridge to open. Gaffer had nothing to do but to wait. He turned the VHS to channel nine to listen to bridge traffic and sat back to relax. This wasn't so bad.

Now that he was sitting at idle he had a moment to check his gauges and make any adjustments he felt necessary. The chart plotter was perfect for what he needed. It was zoomed to a five mile area surrounding his present location. He could see his way out the Port Everglades Inlet and south almost all the way to Hollywood.

Gaffer found the radar confusing. It was a steady display of buildings, boats, and buoys. He took a moment to try and sort things out but did not like what he saw, so he switched it off with a mind to turning it back on after he was outside the inlet. The depth finder was totally wrong. It was set to read the bottom all the way to 800 feet. Gaffer switched the setting to a maximum depth of 100 feet, turned the gain down, and moved the setting to high frequency. Immediately the display turned all blue on the top with an erratic red bottom at about forty feet. This was a more correct setting.

He looked up from the instruments and saw that there was activity on the bridge ahead. He did not hear the bridge bell signaling an opening, probably because he was too far from it to hear, but he could see the red lights flashing on the bridge arm. He eased the controls into forward gear and began moving toward the span. He was in perfect shape to come up behind *Sargasso* and through the span.

The sailboat did not move until both sides of the span were in the full upright position. It was perfectly centered on the opening and began to move forward. *Lady Liberty* was only fifty yards behind the *Sargasso* and Gaffer knew that the bridge would wait for him to go through on the same opening.

In the middle of the span the sailboat made a sudden left turn. Gaffer was watching closely and could see that if the driver did not quickly execute a hard right turn, *Sargasso* was going to crash into the bridge. To Gaffer's horror he saw the sailboat not only not turn right, but it went into reverse. The radio came alive. "Seventeenth Street Bridge, this is sailing yacht *Sargasso*. I have lost control of my steering and can not get through the span. I am in need of immediate assistance."

Adrenaline coursed through Gaffer's body. He went into high alert. The first thing he had to do was to do was look around to assess his options. The outgoing tide was moving *Sargasso* quickly forward and toward the right side of the bridge. It was going to hit hard and possibly do a lot of damage. The current would be unkind if it took hold of *Sargasso* and forced it through the span scraping its side the whole way. Gaffer threw *Lady Liberty* into reverse and picked up the handset before the bridge tender could. He screamed into the mike, "*Sargasso*, this is *Lady Liberty*. I'm right behind you. Quick, put your fenders out and I'll come up behind you and throw you a line." Gaffer had no time for chit chat. "I'm going to do this once so we better get it right."

Immediately the crew on board Sargasso was scurrying around the deck with fenders in hand. Quickly one fender was tied off as the three men on the sailboat held fenders in each hand to keep the boat off the bridge. The bridge tender came on the radio and indicated that he knew there was a problem and would leave the span open. Gaffer had about thirty seconds to figure out what to do. He raced back to the cockpit for a dock line. He fixed it to a cleat on the gunwale and tied two more lengths of line to it. He now had a ninety foot tow rope. He looked ahead and saw that *Sargasso* was jammed against the west wall of the bridge with three crew members trying to push the boat away from the bridge and holding fenders to keep it from crashing or scraping.

Gaffer returned to the helm and looked the situation over. There was easily seventy-five feet of space between the port side of the sailboat and the opposite side of the bridge. He picked up his mike. "*Sargasso*, this is *Lady Liberty*. Do you hear me?"

"That's affirmative," was the only response.

"OK," called Gaffer. "I'm going to pass you on your port side and toss you a line. You better catch it because I have one shot at this. Catch it **and** tie it off a bow cleat and I'll pull you out of there slowly."

A very nervous captain returned to the radio. "I understand. Don't worry, we'll catch it."

Gaffer took two deep breaths to clear his head. He had a large coil of dock line in his hand as he slipped *Lady Liberty* into forward. The boat eased ahead and slowly approached the bridge opening. Gaffer steered wide to the left of the opening and moved forward at no more than three knots. As his boat picked up weigh, he placed one throttle into neutral to slow things down. He looked up and saw his tower looming overhead. This was nerve-wracking. Before he had time to think, he was approaching the bridge opening. Then he was along side of *Sargasso*. The anxious captain had moved to its port side to receive the line, while his two crewmen stayed on the starboard side holding the boat away from the bridge. Gaffer placed *Lady Liberty* into neutral and hurried back to the cockpit. He was almost close enough to the captain of *Sargasso* to hand him the line. He gave it a light toss and it landed across the captain's shoulder. The captain grabbed it tightly in his hand and ran forward to his bow cleat while Gaffer returned to the helm and placed the gear shifts into forward. The boat still had weigh from before Gaffer went to neutral, and it simply continued move forward.

An instant later Gaffer was even with the captain standing on the bow. He was only fifteen feet away. "Are we on?" asked Gaffer.

The captain began some talk about thanks and a bunch of other extraneous jabber. Gaffer interrupted, "We're not out of this yet by a long shot." Insistently he asked, "Are we tied?"

"Yes," replied *Sargasso*'s captain.

Lady Liberty was now passing the sailboat. Gaffer called back, "I'm going to move you out of here slowly, but I can not back up. Get over there with those guys and get busy with the fenders if you don't want to destroy the side of your boat."

With that, *Lady Liberty* cleared the opening of the bridge on the opposite side and the line between the boats became taut. As soon as the line tightened Gaffer could feel *Lady Liberty* being stopped. This was good because he wanted *Sargasso* to lift away from the bridge very slowly. The men on the sailboat felt it move and became very alert with the fenders. By now three fenders were tied off permanently and each man had another in his hand. As *Sargasso* began to move, the men pushed against the bridge and continued to use the fenders.

Gaffer moved in a direction to pull the boat as far away from the bridge as possible. He placed the controls in and out of gear to keep from moving too fast. It was a full two minutes of tugging and maneuvering before *Sargasso* cleared the opposite side of the bridge, but it seemed like an eternity. Gaffer picked up the radio and called the sailboat.

"*Sargasso*, this is *Lady Liberty*. Pick up."

"*Lady Liberty*, *Sargasso*. Thanks again."

"Save it," interrupted Gaffer. "Go to channel twenty-two."

"*Sargasso* switching to channel twenty-two."

On the new channel Gaffer called, "*Sargasso,* you hear me?"

"Loud and clear."

"I'm going to take you ahead two hundred yards to that basin up ahead. Get ready with your anchor."

"Ten-four," came the reply.

Gaffer looked behind and saw two of the crew of *Sargasso* was putting away the fenders while the third was fiddling with the anchor. The way was clear for him to tow the sailboat all the way to the middle of the basin, out of the main channel and safe from traffic. In spite of the tow load behind him, the excitement of the emergency had stretched Gaffer's confidence. He handled the situation well and had handled the boat perfectly. He would never fear a bridge again under normal boating conditions.

It was only five minutes before *Lady Liberty* chugged into the basin and Gaffer was calling back to the sailboat.

"OK, *Sargasso*, we're there. Are you ready?"

"Ready when you are."

Gaffer went to neutral and walked back to the cockpit. The sailboat drifted toward where he was standing but was only moving at about a half knot when it approached *Lady Liberty*. Gaffer reached up and held the sailboat's rail to keep it away from the yacht. "This is it, fellows. Drop your anchor and I'm out of here."

Sargasso's captain thanked him again. "I'm ready."

"OK, then," said Gaffer, "drop your anchor and throw back my dock line."

The captain did as asked and thanked Gaffer for the tenth time. Gaffer felt good about being the Good Samaritan and he also felt good about handling *Lady Liberty* in a tight emergency like that. He wound up the dock lines, tossed them into a corner of the cockpit, and returned to the helm. He placed both controls into forward and idled away from *Sargasso* and out the inlet. He changed the settings on the depth finder to max out at 800 feet, and turned on the radar. Ten minutes later he saw that he was in 200 feet of water. He throttled up to 3,000 RPMs and headed offshore. At 400 feet he plotted a course for Key Biscayne and set the autopilot. The seas were two feet and the sky was clear and blue. It was now 8:30 AM and Gaffer felt like the prince of the world.

TEN

Slight Change of Plans

When Gaffer had piloted Lady Liberty to about three miles offshore, he slowed to idle and then placed the controls into neutral. Calmed in the water, he went below and found a cool soft drink in the refrigerator. He then returned to the helm and continued cruising on a heading of 170 degrees. He sat back in the comfortable captain's chair and surveyed his world. And it was indeed a beautiful place. The bow of the beautiful yacht lay before him, cutting through the light chop. So heavy and powerful was the boat, that he could not even feel the vibration of the small waves being knocked down as the water passed under his keel. All nervousness had left him and he was feeling quite comfortable in control of this beast of a boat. He scanned his controls and gauges and saw that everything was to his liking.

The gentle cruise toward Biscayne Bay had him in a trance. His thoughts wandered here and there, he thought about 'if his friends could see him now'. School crossed his mind but he quickly dispelled that, and then he thought about fishing off *Lady Liberty* and wondered how far Mr. Diamond would let him go when it came to suggesting the right kinds of equipment to put on the boat. He hoped Jeremy did not like to troll too much, and that he could teach him to appreciate bottom fishing.

When Gaffer's cell phone rang he jumped up and his heart raced. It was so unexpected. He took a moment to compose himself and checked the caller ID. Jessica Diamond was on the other end of the line. Gaffer flipped his phone open and greeted her cheerily. "Hi, Jessica. I'll bet you wish you were with me."

Gaffer was startled out of the pleasantness when a near hysterical Jessica Diamond spoke, "Gaffer, I'm sorry. No time to chat. There's been an emergency and we need your help." He was not certain, but Gaffer thought he heard crying.

"What, Mrs. Diamond? Are you all right? Where are you? What's the problem?" Gaffer was now on high alert.

"I don't know if I should even ask you," she said. She was definitely crying. "It's so difficult and I don't know what to do first."

"Calm down and talk to me," said Gaffer. "What's the matter?"

Jessica choked a bit before answering. "My dearest friend just called. She received a ransom demand for her daughter. Her daughter is my god daughter, more like my surrogate niece because I have no children." Jessica was ranting. Gaffer cut her off.

"Mrs. Diamond, slow down. I can't understand what you're saying. Your daughter was kidnaped?"

"No, my friend's daughter." Jessica composed herself and spoke more clearly. "My friends were vacationing in our house in Cat Cay. Their daughter was kidnaped and there has been a ransom demand. We need to go to Cat right away."

"Well, I'm on my way to your house now, I can be there in . . ." Gaffer paused to look on shore to see where he was. It appeared that he had made his way to within a mile of Government Cut in Miami. "Probably less than two hours. You can have the boat and head right out."

"No good, we're in Sarasota right now. A helicopter is picking us up to take us to Miami. It'll take us until at least four this afternoon to get the money. By the time we met you, it would be nearly dark. We want to have the helicopter take us to Cat and for you to meet us there in the boat."

Gaffer was confused. "If you take a helicopter to Cay Cat, why do you need the boat there?"

"Her parents only said bring the boat. It might be an offshore transfer, the girl for the money. We need the boat."

This was much more than Gaffer had bargained for. He had to think about what this meant in his own life and how he could prepare for it. "Give me a minute to think," he said. "Can I call you back in five minutes. I need to call my parents."

"Please, Son, call me back." Jessica used the familiar term 'son' as an expression that Gaffer was the kind of boy she would want for a son if she had one, and also as an endearment so that he would do what he could to help out.

Gaffer clicked off and immediately dialed his father at the office. "Dad."

"Hi, Son. What's up." Max could hear panic in Gaffer's voice.

"Dad, I just received a call from Mrs. Diamond. A friend of theirs was staying in Cat Cay and her daughter was kidnaped. She needs this boat over there as soon as possible and she asked me to take it."

Max did not know what to think. He questioned Gaffer further, "You need to tell me more. Why can't they take the boat over themselves? I mean, don't get me wrong, if there's an emergency we want to help, but is this the only way?"

Gaffer's thoughts were much clearer now. "The Diamonds are in Sarasota. They just got the call and they're hiring a helicopter to bring them to Miami to pick up the ransom money and then to take them to Cat."

"So why do they need you to take the boat?" Max asked.

"I think Mrs. Diamond said the kidnapers want to make the transfer offshore."

"Oh," said Max. "I understand."

"What should I do, Dad?"

"Where are you, Son?"

"I'm about a mile offshore of Government Cut."

"Do you have fuel?"

Gaffer looked at his gauge. "Half full," he said.

"Is that enough to get you there?"

"Who knows? Nobody told me how much fuel this thing burns."

"Let me put you on hold for a minute. Sit tight, I'll be right with you." Max rushed around his office speaking with each department head. He wanted to know if there was any way the office could do without him for a day or two. It was an emergency. Several people asked him to OK this, or stay a couple of minutes to sign something they had to prepare. Since it was an emergency they would make do without him. He returned to his desk and took the telephone off hold. "I'm back. I'm going with you."

"Thanks, Dad. I really didn't want to do this by myself."

"Here's what I want you to do. It'll take me a half hour to get to Miami Beach Marina. Go in there to the fuel dock. Top off the tanks. By the time you're done with that I'll be there."

"Thanks, Dad. That makes me feel much better. I'm going to call Mrs. Diamond and tell her."

"OK, I'll see you soon." Just as he was about to hang up Gaffer came back, "Oh, Dad. What about passports and stuff? Can you take care of that too?"

Max considered for a moment. He tried to think how he could get past that problem when an excellent solution came to him. "I'm going to call Virgil Price. He can help and he has three officers in Bimini who can also help with the kidnaping. Do you have your driver's license on you?"

"Yeah."

"Me too. That'll have to do. I'll see you as soon as possible."

"Thanks, Dad. I'll call Mrs. Diamond and tell her."

They hung up and each of them dialed new numbers. Max called to the headquarters of the Royal Bahamas Defense Force in Nassau, Bahamas. Because the number he called was private, he was connected straight through to the Superintendent of the Defense Force. "Hello, Virgil, this is Max Carson."

Virgil Price was ecstatic to hear from his old friend. Max would have liked to have chatted but he had critical business to discuss. "Virgil, I'm sorry but I have to get right to the point. A friend here in the states has received a ransom demand for their daughter or a friend's daughter, I don't know exactly who it is, but this child has been kidnaped out of Cat Cay and they have asked Gaffer to bring their boat across."

"Slow down, Max," said the superintendent. "You're going too fast."

"I'm sorry, Virgil. I'll start at the beginning. Do you remember the luxury yacht that sank off Cat about two weeks ago?"

"Of course," replied Virgil. "I saw that you were one of the heros."

Max was taken aback. "Where did you hear that?"

"I spoke with Chet Cristy. He told me he saw you in Bimini."

"OK, OK," said Max. "Anyhow, the people we saved took a liking to Gaffer and he is now going to be the mate on their new yacht. They've become friendly. So, Gaffer was out off Miami delivering the boat to their home in Coral Gables when they called and told him about the kidnaping. They want him to bring the boat to Cat instead of to their home. They are collecting the money for the ransom and flying to Cat by helicopter. They need the boat because the demand was for an offshore payment."

Virgil listened patiently until Max was finished. "I have a team in Bimini that can help," he offered.

"Thank you," said Max. "Also, I'm leaving my office now to go meet up with Gaffer in South Beach. He's coming in, fueling, and then I'm boarding there, and we want to go straight over."

"My men will meet you there," said Virgil. "I'm glad you called me, Max. There's a lot we can do, and I want to help."

"Thanks very much Virgil. I've got to go now, there's one other thing."

"Sure, what's that?"

"We're being rushed out of here because of the emergency. Our passports are in Boca and it would take me another two hours to go there and get them. Can your people let us in on our drivers licenses?"

"I'll take care of it. What kind of documentation do you have for the boat?"

"I have no idea, Virgil. It's new to this owner, he just took delivery of it yesterday. It's called *Lady Liberty*."

"OK, I'll take care of it. My men will be in Cat before you can get there."

"Thanks a million," said Max. "This is huge and I appreciate it."

"It's OK, Max. Just go join your son. We can talk later."

They rang off and Max punched another line on his phone. He dialed home. Lisa Carson was not there so the answer machine picked up. Max hung up and dialed Lisa's cell phone. She answered right away.

"Honey, listen, I'm in a huge hurry. Gaffer called and he has been asked to deliver the boat to Cat Cay. It's an emergency, a friend of the Diamond's was kidnaped. They're flying over there later and need the boat there when they get there. It's all worked out. Virgil Price is going to send some men over. Anyhow, I gotta go."

"But wait. What do you mean?"

Lisa was not able to complete her question. Max interrupted. "Listen, I have to leave the office right this minute. To meet up with the boat in South Beach. I'll call you when I get on the road. Gotta go." and he hung up.

The paperwork that Max needed to sign was now ready. He scribbled his signature across four or five pieces of paper and shut down his desktop computer. He said good bye to the office and headed down to the parking garage to hit the road. As soon as he as out from under the building where he could get some reception for his cell phone, he called to Gaffer.

"Where are you now, Son?"

"I'm between the jetties. I'll be at the fuel dock in five minutes or less. Hey Dad, I don't have any money for the fuel."

"I'm on my way. Just fill up and I'll pay when I get there. Is there any food on the boat?"

"Not really," said Gaffer. "There's a small grocery at the dock."

"OK, load up and I'll pay for that too. What's the sea like?"

"Less than three, probably three to five offshore."

"Call Jessica and tell her that we'll be in Cat in about four hours. We have clearance for the boat from Virgil Price and he's sending his men down from Bimini to help out."

"She'll be glad to hear that. I'm going to call her before I try to dock. Then we'll be all set to go." Gaffer hung up and immediately dialed Jessica Diamond's cell phone. Jeremy answered.

"Oh, Jeremy. It's Gaffer."

"Hi, Gaffer. What did you find out?"

"I was just off Miami Beach when Jessica called so I called my father. He's going to meet me at the Miami Beach Marina where I'm going to take on fuel. We'll be in Cat within four hours, no later."

"That's wonderful," said Jeremy. "You don't know how much better that makes me feel. I hated asking you to take the boat over there by yourself."

"I would have done it, but now I don't have to. Also, our good friend is the head of the Defense Force in Nassau. He's sending some officers to Cat Cay. They're in Bimini now and are moving straight over to Cat. They'll be there to meet the boat."

"Hold on," said Jeremy. Gaffer could hear Jeremy telling Jessica what Gaffer had just told him. He came back on the line. "That's wonderful news, Gaffer. Thank you so much for this, and please thank you dad for us too. We'll see you in a little while." After a brief hesitation he added, "And don't worry about what ever you have to spend on the boat. I'll take care of it when I see you later."

"OK, then," said Gaffer. "I'll just see you later."

"Thanks again, Gaffer, Thanks a million."

"OK, OK. You're welcome." Gaffer hung up and placed the phone on the seat next to him. He steered up to the fueling dock at Miami Beach Marina and slowed to a stop. Across forty feet of water he called to the dock master. "Can I get some diesel?"

The dock master waved him into the dock. Gaffer eased closer, and then a little closer. From a distance of six feet away he tossed over first a spring line, then a bow line, then the stern line. The dock was well protected so Gaffer decided not to put out the fenders. When the lines were secure, Gaffer shut down the main engines. He left the generator running and climbed across to the dock.

While Max raced down I 95 to the MacArthur Causeway, Gaffer was fueling *Lady Liberty*. It took four hundred gallons of diesel. When the gauges read a bit higher than three quarters, Gaffer stopped the pump and handed the nozzle back across to the attendant. He then entered the grocery store and bought at least two of everything he thought might be useful. He also bought six cases of Cokes and ten of bottled water. He bought plenty of milk, coffee, cereals, lunch meats, bread, and every kind of condiment. While he was there he also picked up a sturdy long handled brush, three plastic buckets, two bottles of liquid detergent, spot remover, two chamois, six rolls of paper towels, a container of RainX, and two fifty foot long dock hoses with nozzles.

The store's small fishing department had little of interest for a serious fisherman, but Gaffer was able to pick up three knives of different sizes for cleaning fish. As he began to look around, he knew immediately that there were a few other things he might be able to use. He could not bear the thought of being in Bimini waters with no possible way to hook a fish. He selected two inexpensive matched rods and spinning reel outfits in the twelve pound class. They were already spooled with monofilament line. He picked up three packs of Mustad stainless steel hooks, a dozen 4/0's, another dozen size 6/0, and a dozen 7/0's. The boat could always use more hooks. He bought several packs of various sized snap swivels and two packages of sabiki rigs for live baiting. He then move over to the freezer where he took out three five pound boxes of frozen squid, a dozen rigged ballyhoo, a dozen unrigged ballyhoo, two five pound boxes of frozen silver sides, and two five pound boxes of frozen chum. It was a modest beginning for *Lady Liberty*, but he had to start somewhere.

The dock master was very obliging when Gaffer told him that his father would be along soon to pay. He and his assistant helped Gaffer to load everything on the boat. While they waited Gaffer stored the groceries and cleaning supplies. When that was done he topped off the water tank and then walked down the dock to see if any of the charter boats had gotten lucky that day. Four out of six of the fleet were flying sail fish flags upside down in the universal sign of release. One of the boats was flying three flags, one was flying two, and the other two were each flying one flag.

It was 1:00 PM when Max pulled into the Miami Beach Marina parking lot. He brought with him whatever he had handy in the way of changes of clothes. Fortunately he had his gym bag with him which could supply him with a couple of pairs of gym shorts, a couple more tee shirts, and a pair of running shoes that would suffice as deck shoes. In the small store he bought two tee shirts each for himself and Gaffer, and two large brimmed hats to help keep the sun off their heads. He picked up as much in the way of toiletries as he and Gaffer would need. He knew that in Cat Cay he would be able to buy whatever more he needed to make it through the time they were there.

Max handed his American Express card over to the dock master. The total bill was $1,163. Max signed the receipt and placed it and his card into his wallet. Gaffer climbed up to the helm and started the big diesel engines. He switched on all the instruments and watched the fuel indicator move nearly to the full mark. The water indicator did the same. Max stood on the deck waiting for the dock master to toss over the dock lines. When that was done he wound the lines up and stored them in their rightful place in the cockpit. He pushed with all his might against the dock and *Lady Liberty* moved about eight feet off. Gaffer backed away from the dock and performed his patented 180. He then went to forward gear and headed toward the Cut. Max went below and immediately changed out of his work clothes and street shoes. He opted for shorts, a tee shirt and bare feet. When he was comfortable and had a cold beer from the refrigerator, he ascended the stairs to the helm area. He took a seat next to his son and pulled out his cell phone. After calls were made to his wife, more fully explaining the emergency situation for which they were recruited, and then to the Diamonds to let them know they were on their way, he sat back next to his son and watched him in his new role as sea captain.

CHAPTER ELEVEN

Kidnaped at Cat

The golf carts whirred to a stop at the ocean front home of Jeremy and Jessica Diamond. It was not Cat Cay's largest home, but it was by far the most beautifully kept. Its garden of colorful bougainvillea and hibiscus, along with the fragrant orange jasmine and brightly blooming impatiens, would have been difficult to maintain in the best of soil, much more so in the sandy soil of the islands. Tall pine trees shaded most of the grounds, keeping the property uncommonly cool in the warm tropical climate. The paint was fresh, bright white with aqua and salmon trim. The walkways were swept clean, and expensive date palm trees lined the walkway leading up to the front porch. The view from the rear patio looked out over one of the island's only private pool terraces, with Cat Cay's most perfect sandy beach in front, and the Gun Cay Lighthouse just across the cut beyond that.

Jordan and Abbey Deere were shocked to hear the loud pounding on the door. They had learned earlier in the day that their daughter was in the hands of, who knew who, and they were being blackmailed for a great sum of money for her return. When Jordan Deere answered the door, he was positive that the kidnapers had come to create more trouble. His heart was beating wildly as he timidly opened the door a crack. Cameron stepped forward and took the lead.

"Mr. Deere, I am Cameron Ford of the Royal Bahamas Defense

Force, here to investigate a report about a kidnaping. Please let us in."

Jordan Deere relaxed. The relief nearly caused him to faint. He opened the door to permit the men to enter and introduced himself and his wife. Cameron introduced the four other men and came right to the point.

"I want to know everything about this kidnaping. What did they say? What are they demanding?"

"Could I ask you, how did you know about this? We told no one about it."

Max and Gaffer looked surprised. "You didn't tell Jeremy Diamond?"

"Oh, that. Yes, this is his home. I called him right away when we heard from the kidnapers. He's the only one I told. How did the police find out?"

The men all took seats in the large living room. Max explained about the call from Jessica Diamond to Gaffer, who in turn called his father, who in turn called Virgil Price. From that chain of phone calls things started happening.

"Tell me everything from the beginning," said Cameron. "Don't leave anything out."

"We received a call. . ." began Jordan Deere. He was immediately interrupted.

"When," demanded Cameron.

"About nine o'clock this morning," stammered Jordan.

"What's your daughter's name? How old is she?"

"Eleven," said Abbey Deere. "Her name is Kathryn. We call her Kate." For the first time all day Mrs. Deere felt like something was being done about this horrible situation. She broke down in tears.

Cameron turned back to Jordan. "What happened? When did you last see your daughter?"

"She left at about eight to go to the club house. She likes to walk the docks in the morning. It's OK with us. We always thought of Cat Cay as a safe place."

"Don't start beating yourself up yet," said Cameron. "You need to hold yourself together. I want to know everything you know, every detail. When and how did you find out about the abduction?"

"About an hour after Kate left we received a telephone call. It was a man's voice, deep, Bahamian accent. He said he had my daughter, he let her say 'Daddy' and he took the phone away from her. He said we had until tomorrow night to get five hundred thousand dollars if we ever wanted to see our daughter again. He said get the money, get a boat, and be ready by tomorrow night. He told us not to call the police."

Abbey was sobbing openly. Cameron was sympathetic but firm. "Mrs. Deere, it will do no good for you to fall apart now. We need all the resources we can find to get your daughter back, so I suggest you pull yourself together."

She buried her head in her hands and cried. She could not make herself stop, she could only think the worst, that she might never again see her little girl, her only child.

"What else can you tell me? Have you seen anybody taking an unhealthy interest in your daughter or yourself? Anyone?"

"I'm sorry, Mr. Ford. This is our first vacation in Cat Cay. We don't know anybody here or who is supposed to be here or who is not. Everybody is a stranger to us."

"Just so you know," said Cameron, "this is not the first kidnaping to happen in this area. In fact, it's the third in six months. It's a serial kidnaping, and we can not allow that to continue."

Sheer panic crossed Abbey Deere's face. Hysterically she asked, not certain she really wanted to know, "How did they work out? Was anybody hurt? Will we get our daughter back?"

"All of the incidents ended with the kidnaped parties being returned safely. In each instance the families failed to contact the police and in each instance a ransom was paid. We believe this is the work of one group, but we have no idea who it is. Our goal is to be involved in this from the beginning and catch the kidnapers."

Max said, "The Diamonds are in Miami collecting the money for the ransom. They should be here any time now. In the worst case, this will cost you the money but you'll have your little girl back."

That was intended to calm Mrs. Deere if she could hear through her sobs. Cameron made a plan with his men. "There can't be more than two hundred people on this island. I want to round them all up and question every one of them. I want to know who might have seen the girl, who has seen anybody new on the island, any strange boats, anything. Bring everyone down to the marina. Knock on doors, stop people on the paths, get them off the golf course. Everyone in the marina in one hour. Spread out, the island is not that big. Chet and Cecil, if anybody refuses, you have my permission to threaten to arrest them. Max and Gaffer, you just try to be persuasive and let them know how important this is. Most people will want to cooperate. Mr. and Mrs. Deere, you can help too. It's not doing you any good to sit here worrying. Get involved, it will make you feel like you are doing something."

The entire group poured out of the house and took off in seven directions. The Defense Force officers moved briskly in a direction more or less toward the marina. Gaffer took off at a run to knock on doors at the opposite end of the island. He had been to Cat Cay several times and knew the island fairly well. He knew that a half mile to the south there were twenty or thirty houses to contact. Max tried to trot behind him but could not keep up. Mrs. and Mrs. Deere headed out to the golf course.

Surprisingly there was a very high degree of cooperation. The instant they were told of the emergency, the residents stopped what they had been doing and hurried down to the marina. It took an hour before Gaffer and Max had completed the rounds of the homes and then they walked the last 200 yards to the marina. As they passed the last home and made their way into the extreme southern end of the dock area, the thunderous sound of the Bell Jet Ranger Helicopter filled the air. It came in fast and reckless and landed on the first tee of the golf course. When it settled down on solid ground, the engines slowed and finally died. A minute later Jeremy and Jessica Diamond emerged from the helicopter and moved briskly toward the club house. Jordan and Abbey Deere ran out to meet them. They hugged and talked a mile a minute as they walked off the golf course.

"The gathering is at the marina," said Jordan. "The whole island is there. They have all come out to help."

"OK, then," said Jeremy. "We go to the marina." They changed course and in five minutes were joining the rest of the island crowd.

Cameron Ford stood on the rear cargo platform of one of the golf carts. He was surrounded by 150 residents and employees of the Cat Cay resort. He saw inquisitive faces, eager to hear the facts as they were known, not more of the rumor mill that had been stirred up in the past hour or so.

For the most part they knew that there had been a kidnaping and that there had been a ransom demand. The helicopter was a rare occurrence, as was the rousting of the members from their homes. The island was on high alert.

"This morning sometime between eight and nine o'clock a young girl named Kate Deere was taken from the island," said Cameron in a voice loud enough to be heard at the back of the crowd. "The people who took her have contacted her parents and made a ransom demand. We have reason to believe these people have left the island by boat. We called you here to ask each one of you if you saw anything unusual in the marina, or anywhere on the island today at about that time."

One by one the residents and employees of the club described what they could remember in the way of activity around the marina. Every boat that came and went was described. Some were known by their names, some had been seen before, a few had never been seen before this day. But the marina at Cat Cay was a busy place where dozens of boats came and left each day. For the most part, unless a craft was a particular model that attracted attention, boats came and went with little notice. Because Cat Cay was a resort, few people including the staff could tell which faces were familiar and which ones were new.

Cameron was becoming exhausted from people asking questions when he really had no good answers. A hand in the back of the crowd shot up to be recognized. Cameron pointed at the woman wearing the uniform of an island housekeeper.

"I was cleaning the Turkel residence on the southwest point and saw a group of people get into a boat that had been beached. They pushed it back out into the water and took off to the northwest."

127

"Did you see a little girl with them," asked Cameron.

"I couldn't tell. I only had a quick look, but I thought about how strange that someone would go there with a boat instead of to the marina."

"That could be an important lead. Can you describe the boat or any of the people on it?" asked Cameron.

The crowd moved aside so the woman could approach the golf cart. "I know nothing about boats. I'm sorry. I think it was white or gray."

"I'm sure you can tell me more," said Cameron. "Did it have outboard engines, could you tell that? Was it big? Could you see the seats or a cabin?"

The woman closed her eyes trying to picture the boat in her head. She took her time because she did not want to make a mistake. "I don't know about the engines, but it was open, I mean, no cabin." She tried to picture the scene again, and after a moment added, "I think there were four people all together, and I think they were black men."

"No little girl?" asked Cameron.

"I just don't know," said the woman.

Another woman, this one a resident remembered something. "I don't know if this is important, but our golf cart was missing this morning. We live near the Diamond's home and we found it close to the Turkel residence. I'll bet that's who moved it."

"Of course," said Cameron. "Now that's the kind of information we are looking for. That could easily have been the kidnaper's transportation. Who else has something?"

A teenage boy spoke up. "I saw that golf cart heading to Turkel's. I saw it!"

"What can you tell us?" asked Jeremy Diamond.

"It had three people on it is all I know. I thought it was strange because I know your cart," he was speaking to the woman who had lost her cart. "I wondered for a minute why workmen would be using a private cart instead of one of the work carts."

"How did you know they were workmen?" asked Cameron.

The boy was embarrassed to respond. "It's just that almost all of the black men on this island are workers and most of the residents are white." He hated saying that to Cameron who himself was a black man. He did not want to appear racist. It was just a commonly known fact that the residential population of the island were white folks, mostly from South Florida, and most of the black population of the island were staff members.

Cameron sensed the boy's embarrassment. "That's very good. That's the kind of deduction we need. You see something out of the ordinary and that can give us a clue."

The boy looked visibly relieved that Cameron had not been offended. Nor did it seem that the remark phased Cecil Hunter or Chet Christy who were also black. Cameron continued with the boy, "Did you happen to see the young girl with them on the cart?"

"I'm sorry, Officer, but I didn't get that good of a look."

"OK, very good," said Cameron. "Anybody else? Anything? Did anybody else see the boat." No one responded. "How about the golf cart or the men?" Still no response. The crowd began to mill around and talk among themselves. It appeared that this would be all the information they would be able to collect from this group. Cameron thanked everyone for attending the meeting and asked that they keep their eyes open for the boat, the men, the little girl, anything.

The Diamonds, Carsons, Deeres, and Cameron and his two men

129

walked slowly toward the fuel dock at the end of the pier. *Lady Liberty* was tied there, sitting pretty, ready for action. Jeremy Diamond looked up and saw his new yacht. He stole a moment from the deeply depressing mood of the moment to contemplate his own good fortune in life. The boat made him smile. To him it was the most perfectly suited yacht he could imagine. He put his arm around Gaffer's shoulder and thanked him for bringing the boat across. He shook Max's hand and congratulated him for having such a good boy. He then stepped back to walk along side Cameron. "Lieutenant Ford, thank you for being here for my good friends, the Deeres. I don't know how you got here so fast but I want you to know how much we appreciate it."

"That's our job," said Cameron. "You don't have to thank me. Your bringing the ransom money will be a big help. We now know this will have a better chance of a good ending. We are expecting a call tonight with further instructions."

"Just tell me what I can do to help and I'll do it. The Deeres are our closest friends and Katie is like a daughter to us."

"What are your plans with respect to staying or leaving. Do you intend to be in Cat for a while?"

"I'm not going anywhere until that girl is safely with her parents. I don't care if it takes all winter."

"I'd like to ask another favor if you don't mind," said Cameron.

"Anything," said Jeremy. "Anything, just ask."

"Your boat might come in handy," said Cameron. "I don't know how just yet, but if we had it at our disposal, there's a good chance it will help."

"It's all yours," said Jeremy. "I'll have the fuel topped off and make certain it has everything you need. You and your men are welcome to move onto it and use it as a base if you like."

Cameron moved up toward where Gaffer and Max were walking together. "Mr. Diamond just offered us his boat for this operation. Is that good with you?"

"Of course," said Max. "We want to cooperate any way we can. If **you** need the boat, we'll just catch a ride home in that helicopter."

A quizzical look crossed Cameron's face. "You didn't understand, Max. None of us know how to run that boat. I wouldn't even know how to start it. I meant to use the boat with your help."

"Hold on," said Max. "Let's see what Jeremy had in mind. Maybe he wants to run the boat." They turned around and Max addressed Jeremy, "We brought your boat here, but our plans after that are up in the air. Now Cameron says he and his men are going to use the boat and they want me and Gaffer to run it. How do you want it?"

"Let's talk about it Max," said Jeremy. "I was only thinking that I ought to stay in my house with Jerome and Abbey. They are distraught and I feel like I ought to be with them."

Max nodded his understanding. He had not thought about that. "Give me two minutes to think about it," he said. He took Gaffer aside to get his take on the situation.

"I want to help," said Gaffer. "I want to run the boat. We should both do that and let the Diamonds stay in their house. I think that's the best way we can help."

Max considered for a moment. He looked over at his good friend Cameron Ford whom he knew would be lost if he refused to stay and help. There was nothing more to think about. Max returned to where Jeremy and

Cameron were standing waiting for his decision. "OK, we're in," he said. "What's next?"

"For right now I'm going to stay here at the Diamond's house until we get the call from the kidnapers. I want you to take Cecil and Chet over to Bimini so they can snoop around there. I have a feeling that the little girl is either on North or South Bimini. Think about it, these are the only inhabited islands around here. They are most certainly not on Cat. Bimini seems like the most likely place."

"OK, then, let's go," said Max. "Give your men their orders. We can be ready to shove off within thirty minutes." To Gaffer he said, "Let's top off the fuel and single up the lines. We're heading out."

Gaffer trotted ahead and told the dock master he needed fuel right away. When the dock master turned and saw that the whole group was beginning to move more quickly, he hurried and handed the fuel nozzle to Gaffer. Jeremy Diamond explained to the dock master that the yacht was his and to put all of its expenses on his club account. That settled, the tanks were topped off and Gaffer moved to the helm to start the engines. He switched on the electronics and turned the radar to a twelve mile sweep. Max untied the bow and stern lines so the boat was fixed to the dock by only the spring line. For the ten minutes it would take to board Chet and Cecil, a single spring line would suffice. Cameron gave some last minute instructions to his men before they climbed aboard *Lady Liberty*.

Cameron walked back down the pier with the Diamonds and Deeres. When Max and Cecil pushed away from the dock, Gaffer placed both controls into forward gear. The boat moved to the center of the basin. Cameron turned away to watch. He said to Jeremy Diamond, "Watch this."

The group turned their attention to see Gaffer perform a 180 degree turn within the length of the boat. Sitting in one spot at the slowest possible pace, *Lady Liberty* turned, showed its starboard beam and then continued the slow spin. Jeremy watched his beautiful machine perform. "Nobody does that like the Gaffer," said Cameron. "It's a beautiful thing to watch."

"I take it my boat is in good hands," said Jeremy.

"The best," said Cameron as he led his group past the club house and down the path to the Diamond residence.

The sun was at a sharp angle to the horizon as *Lady Liberty* passed through Gun Cay Cut. Gaffer held his hand in front of his face to block his eyes from its bright light. On his radar display he could clearly see Bimini and all the small islands in between. Past the lighthouse he turned to 300 degrees and throttled up to twenty-eight knots. Five minutes later at the 600 foot mark on his depth finder, he turned to 360 degrees. By the estimate on his GPS he would be in Bimini in twenty-two minutes.

TWELVE

Bimini Twist

On the ride up to Bimini from Cat Cay a sketchy plan was hatched. Gaffer would drop Chet and Cecil off at Bimini Sands Marina and from there they would snoop around the island to see what information they could pick up. They would question everyone they encountered, asking if they had seen several black men accompanying a little girl. It was not much to go on, but small clues were usually better than none at all. They would give themselves until 11:00 PM, five hours, and then they would find *Bimini Twist* at the dock that Max had described to them, and bring it back to North Bimini. Gaffer and Max would continue on to North Bimini, a distance of only four hundred yards, and dock at Sea Crest. From there they would go on foot to the different marinas along the waterfront asking dock masters and anyone else they came across for information about the kidnappers. Somebody had to have seen something. It was a weak plan, but it beat doing nothing.

There were no boats docked in the Bimini Sands Marina that fit the description of the boat that had been beached at Cat Cay. Cecil and Chet walked over to the dock office and called on the manager and the resident customs officer. They explained the situation and asked for any leads the men might have. No one had seen anything. However, the customs officer offered to help in the search. He joined Chet and Cecil in knocking on the doors of the Bimini Sands residents to see what they might know. It took an hour to complete canvassing the oceanfront townhouses before the three men turned their attention elsewhere. Rather than walk around the miles of sparsely populated roads on the island, the men opted to find *Bimini Twist* and patrol the island by its waterways. The greater number of homes were to be found on the canals, and this was the only possible place that boat could be, if it were anywhere at all on South Bimini.

"Chet, are you going to recognize *Bimini Twist* when we see it?" asked Cecil.

"It's been a while since I've seen it," said Chet. "But I remember that it's an open fisherman, about twenty-five feet long with a center console and two outboards. It also has the name on the side in letters about a foot high and ten feet long. We'll know it right away when we see it."

The two men climbed into the Customs Officer's jeep and rode out to the canal in which *Bimini Twist* was said to be docked. When they arrived there was no question. *Bimini Twist* was the only boat in the canal. Chet took the dock lines while Cecil started the engines. In five minutes they were cruising the canals of South Bimini

When Captain Jake saw that it was Max and Gaffer on *Lady Liberty*, he gave them their favorite slip. They spent twenty minutes docking the boat and securing it in its slip. Bow, stern, and spring lines were secured, and the shore power was hooked up. Gaffer turned off the engines and the generator. Oh, the beautiful silence. They invited Captain Jake on board *Lady Liberty* first to explain the situation relating to the kidnaping, and second to show off the boat. It was now past dark and Max and Gaffer had skipped lunch. They would soon hit the waterfront and question everyone in sight, but not before they grabbed a quick bite to eat at C.J.'s Deli.

Captain Jake could not help them. A hundred or more boats passed by Sea Crest on the slowest of days, and he rarely noticed any of them. He might have paid attention if he had seen three or four black men walking with a reluctant little girl, but he had not seen anything like that. The three men headed over to C.J.'s. Over a quick hamburger they made a plan for canvassing the island. The best they figured they could do was to hit all the motels and all the marinas in Alicetown. It would take a while but it would not be that difficult to do. They gulped down dinner and headed north on Kings Highway to conduct some interviews.

Jake knew every dockmaster on the island, so he called on them while Max and Gaffer knocked on the office of every motel they could find. It took time to tell the story to everyone they saw, but they had to do it if they were to get the word out and pick up any clues. The five main motels up to the Big Game Club were checked, as were any marinas, bars, or restaurants associated with them. This only took an hour and a half so Max and Gaffer continued north on Kings Highway and visited the bars and restaurants more typically frequented by the Bimini locals.

"It starts to get a little crazy the farther north you go," said Gaffer. "Are you sure you want to go up there?"

"What do you mean?" asked his father. "You don't like it up there?"

"I don't go up there enough to know," said Gaffer.

"Then let's go. I'll bet you find the people nicer and more cooperative than anywhere else. I've been up there plenty of times and it has always been good."

Jake had to return to his duties in the marina, so Max and Gaffer spent the next two hours talking to Bimini locals anywhere they could find them. Max was right, they tried to be helpful, they were courteous, and very concerned for the welfare of the little girl. Unfortunately nobody had any clues for them, and they ended up heading back toward Sea Crest knowing no more than they knew when they left Cat Cay four hours earlier.

Upon arriving back at the marina they noticed that *Bimini Twist* was docked in one of the slips. Gaffer climbed down into it as Max continued on down the dock toward *Lady Liberty*. Gaffer shined a flash light onto the deck of his boat only to see that it was filthy with two weeks of salt grime, mixed with Chet and Cecil's dirty footprints. He shined his light into the storage space of the center console and found the boat soap. He poured about a half cup into a three gallon bucket and then climbed back onto the dock and attached his fifty foot hose to the fresh water spigot. He turned the water on and jumped back into *Bimini Twist*. He filled the bucket with water and gave the entire boat a quick spray with the fresh water hose. For the next twenty minutes he scrubbed with the long handled brush. He could not see all the foot prints and other dirt as it was now past midnight and pitch black darkness, so he scrubbed everything, not missing a single square inch. First he scrubbed the front half of the boat from the tip of the bow to the center console. He then rinsed the soap off and allowed it to flow down and out the scuppers. He turned the fresh water hose on the inside of the T-top and gave a light spray to the console and its instruments. He allowed that to drip while he scrubbed the back area of the boat from the center console to the transom. He even gave a good brushing to the engines as best as he could reach them. After he made a few passes along the waterline with his brush, he dumped the soapy water over the side, rinsed the bucket and then sprayed the rest of the soap away. He shined the flash light around the boat to see how much better it looked. It was not the best job he had ever done, but he knew he would not be able to sleep well if he were thinking that *Bimini Twist* was sitting only a few slips away and somebody might see it in the morning looking like it had been neglected. Gaffer spent another ten minutes wiping the water off the bow deck, the gunwales, the center console. He was particularly careful to wipe all the water off his instrument panel. He hung his wet towel over the whale tail of the leaning post and climbed out of the boat. He then wound up his hose and turned off the fresh water. Five minutes later he entered the cabin of *Lady Liberty* listening to the report from Cecil Hunter.

The kidnappers had called the Deere family at 10:00 PM. Jordan told them that the money was ready and that they would meet them anywhere, any time. He was told to be prepared to make the drop the following night, somewhere in the vicinity of Highborne Cay. Everyone was surprised by that revelation. Highborne Cay was what, a hundred miles away in the Exuma chain of islands. No wonder they were unable to learn anything by scouring the Bimini waterfront. They were way off base.

Cameron instructed them to get ready to cast off again. As soon as Max and Gaffer returned to the boat they were to take off again and head across the Great Bahama Bank. Gaffer had not even had a chance to take a seat in the galley when he was told to get ready. He was exhausted from a very long and tiring day, but his curiosity and excitement about traveling to the Exumas gave him new energy.

Max was concerned for his son. "Gaffer, you need to get some sleep. I'll drive us to Highborne."

"Let me take the first hour," said Gaffer. "I'll get us out of the marina and onto the bank. Then I'll program the autopilot for our destination. From that, anybody can take the wheel and just make sure we don't run over anything on the way, and I'll set the radar."

"Did you happen to notice how much fuel there is on *Bimini Twist?*" asked Max.

"I didn't turn on the instruments. I have no idea."

"I saw it," said Chet. "Just over half."

"Are you thinking of taking it with us?" asked Gaffer.

"I'm not thinking about it, we're doing it."

"But what about the gas?" asked Gaffer.

"We'll tow it." answered Max. "This boat is so big and strong, you won't even know it's back there."

"Good," said Gaffer. "There's no reason not to take it. You go get it ready and I'll get this boat ready. We can leave in fifteen minutes."

"Let's do it," said Max. He climbed off *Lady Liberty* and walked down the dock to where *Bimini Twist* was sitting in its slip. Without starting the engines he untied all the dock lines and unhooked the fresh water hose. He jumped in the boat and put the hose back in its storage compartment. When he was sure everything was secured for the trip across the Bahama Bank, he started the engines and idled out into the channel. While he waited for Lady Liberty to join him, he rigged a tow harness to the two cleats and tow ring on the bow. He used the anchor line which had a 3/4 inch diameter and was 200 feet long.

Chet and Cecil untied Lady Liberty from the dock and disconnected the shore power cord. They brought in all the lines and utilities and pushed away from the pier. Chet took in the fenders while Cecil walked back to the stern to get ready to receive the tow rope. Gaffer eased the controls into forward and moved the boat out into the channel. Max brought *Bimini Twist* back around to the stern of *Lady Liberty*. When he was within ten feet of the other boat he tossed the line to Cecil. "Pull me in," he said.

Cecil pulled *Bimini Twist* the last ten feet and held it off as Max climbed onto *Lady Liberty's* transom. He pushed *Bimini Twist* back and took the line from Cecil. He took three crossing wraps on the cleat and then locked the line down. Gaffer was patiently waiting at the helm for the men to complete this job and come join him. He looked at *Bimini Twist* and called back to his father. "Did you mean to run with the anchor light on?"

Max looked back. He had meant to turn that light on, but forgot all about it. "Hold on," he said as he pulled on the tow rope and brought *Bimini Twist* up. He crossed again with Cecil's help and within thirty seconds had turned the lights on and was climbing back on board the yacht. He called to his son, "We can go now."

Gaffer put the controls in forward and idled out until the line between the two boats became taut. *Bimini Twist* swung around and followed. Cecil and Chet both had strong flashlights trained to the rear and could see that *Bimini Twist* seemed to be riding well. *Lady Liberty* cleared the harbor and throttled up to fifteen knots. Everything to the rear still looked good, so Gaffer held it at fifteen knots until he cleared the bend at the tip of South Bimini. Chet and Cecil kept their lights on *Bimini Twist* and Gaffer powered up to twenty-five knots. Still *Bimini Twist* seemed to be riding well, so they turned off their lights and came up to the helm. Gaffer and Max were programming the chart plotter and autopilot for a heading toward Highborne Cay. They determined that the distance was 140 miles and they figured to get there by sunup. With the autopilot and radar to guide them they decided on one and a half hour watches on the helm. The image of *Bimini Twist* in the radar was a huge green splash at the bottom of the X in the middle of the screen. As long as that stayed right where it was they knew there was nothing to worry about.

Gaffer stayed at the helm for about fifteen minutes. He was amazed to find that *Lady Liberty* was no slower at 3,300 RPM's towing *Bimini Twist* than it was without it. When he was finally satisfied that everything was under control, he turned the helm over to Cecil Hunter and headed toward his bunk. Max and Chet were also bushed and within another thirty minutes they too were fast asleep.

At 1:00 AM Cecil went below and shook Chet awake. "Sorry, Buddy, but it's your watch."

Chet's feet immediately hit the floor and he was out of his bunk. "Give me a second," he said as he used the head to relieve himself and throw water on his face. He then followed Cecil out to the helm where he was shown around the instrument panel and controls. It was all quite straight forward, and while Chet had some knowledge of boating and nautical instruments, this particular yacht was very sophisticated and took some getting used to. After figuring out about enough to make it through the night safely, they decided to contact Cameron for an update.

Cecil keyed in his high powered portable radio set and called out. The radio protocol was informal and brief, "Cameron, are you monitoring? This is Cecil."

It took only a few seconds for a response. "Cecil, where are you?"

Cecil referred to the chart plotter on his instrument panel. "We're about thirty-five or forty miles out of Bimini. Everything is good here. How about you?"

"We decided to stay here in Cat until the morning. We'll leave here sometime between eight and ten AM. We're waiting for one more call from the kidnappers and then we're going to take off."

"All right," said Cecil. "We'll be making our way to Highborne. We should be arriving by about sunrise. We'll just tie up in the marina and wait for you there."

"I'll call you just before we take off," said Cameron. "When you get there look around for the boat rental place. I think you can rent a skiff."

"We have one," replied Cecil. "We're towing *Bimini Twist.*" He turned to Chet, "Shine your light back there and make certain that it's still back there."

Chet pointed to the large green splash at the bottom or the radar screen. "Right there," he said.

Cecil nodded. Cameron replied, "Good, *Bimini Twist.* That's perfect for what we need. Call me when you get to Highborne."

They clicked off their radios and Cecil went below for some shuteye while Chet sat back to relax at the helm. Before now he had not paid much attention to all the controls, screens and gauges. He considered how difficult it would be to run this boat if he did not have the preset autopilot and radar. He had a look around with his night vision binoculars but there was nothing to see. He turned his flashlight to the rear and saw that *Bimini Twist* was riding well. That was it as far as responsibilities went, so he sat back for a boring hour and a half watch.

By 6:45 AM everybody was up. Gaffer was at the helm and the sun was just about to peek out from beyond the horizon. For the last thirty miles they would be off the Great Bahama Bank where the water averaged only about fifteen feet of depth. They entered the Tongue of the Ocean where waters ranged as deep as 2,000 feet and more. Gaffer's mind went to thoughts of how good he had heard the fishing was in this area. He stuck his head down into the salon and called to his father.

"Dad, come here a minute."

Max walked out onto the deck and gazed over to where a sliver of bright orange sun was showing above the eastern horizon. He took the seat along side his son and breathed in the fresh air. "Nice out here, huh?"

"A little cool, but it's going to be a beautiful day," said Gaffer. "I wanted to ask you. This is my first visit to the Tongue. We're ahead of schedule and I was thinking about taking the *Twist* and towing a bait the rest of the way to Highborne."

Max considered for a minute and could think of no reason not to. "Do you have everything you need?"

"I have a couple of rods on the *Twist*, and there are two new spinning outfits on the Viking. There's some rigged ballyhoo and we have about ten artificial lures on our boat."

"Then let's do it," said Max. He went below to let Chet and Cecil know that he and Gaffer were leaving. This caught their attention as neither of them felt competent to bring *Lady Liberty* safely into Highborne Cay. Because of their nervousness about the situation, Max agreed to allow Cecil to fish off *Bimini Twist* with Gaffer while he stayed aboard the Viking with Chet and navigated to their final destination.

Gaffer throttled down while Max stood on the dive platform and pulled *Bimini Twist* up to *Lady Liberty*. Gaffer retrieved a half dozen frozen ballyhoos and the two spinning rods. He did not bother with hooks or leaders as his own boat was loaded with that kind of equipment. He stood on the gunwale and climbed across. Cecil handed the fishing gear to Gaffer and crossed over himself. The first thing that Gaffer did was to start the engines and allow then to warm up. While the engines warmed he tied snap swivels onto the two rods and skirted ballyhoos before completing his rigs.

143

Chet untied *Bimini Twist* from the cleat on *Lady Liberty* and tossed the line to Cecil. Gaffer started idling away as Cecil wound up the anchor line and stowed it in the anchor locker.

Max sat at the helm of *Lady Liberty* and placed the throttles into forward. He moved a hundred yards away before Gaffer was ready to put *Bimini Twist* into gear. Max's radio came alive. "*Lady Liberty, Bimini Twist,* radio check."

"Loud and clear," came the response. "Gaffer, I'm going to stay with you. We're in no hurry and once they start biting, I want my share."

Gaffer laughed. "You get the third hookup," he responded.

"I'll take it," said Max. "Call me when it's my turn."

Gaffer payed out two lines behind the boat. He wanted to have a four line spread but he had no outriggers. He settled for three. When the baits were sliding beautifully through the water in *Bimini Twist's* wake, Gaffer sat back and waited for the action to begin.

THIRTEEN

Rogue Bull

The helicopter touched down on the flat tarmac usually reserved for the seaplane that landed daily at Highborne Cay. The pilot turned its engines off before the passengers deplaned. It may have been a bitter cold winter in the northern United States, but here in the Exuma chain the weather was perfect. A cold front that had made its way through the island chain two days earlier had left behind clear skies, temperatures in the high seventies, and a gentle breeze out of the northeast. Jordan and Abbey Deere had no time to enjoy, or even notice this beautiful weather, or the pristine beauty of Highborne Cay. They were frantic to be reunited with their daughter and would get no rest or comfort until she was returned to them safely.

Ten miles to the south, Katie Deere sat with her hands tied behind her back in the abandoned ruins of what had at one time been an airplane hangar for a notorious drug lord. Normans Cay gained its infamous reputation during the 1980's when it served as the base for one of the world's most notorious smugglers. When the drug operation was brought down and the kingpin was placed in a U.S. jail, the island compound was abandoned and maintenance ceased. Only remnants of what had once been a luxurious island paradise still remained. But its reputation as a dark spot on the map stayed with it.

Spencer "Axle" Wolfe and his jailhouse buddy, Ron Brown, known by fellow inmates as Stingray, met in the institution in Nassau known as Fox Hill. They were both released a year earlier and drifted around the Bimini and Exuma chains of islands. They were not particularly looking for gainful employment at the time, they were more interested in making a fast buck. Neither man had a reputation for being violent; they were just petty thieves trying to make a couple of big scores. Stingray's distant cousin, Michael "Tiny" Regan, was a hapless, unemployed, undereducated drifter. A very large man at six feet five and weighing just under 300 pounds, he was gentler than he appeared. He could be intimidating, but had never been known to be violent. These were the men who had captured and stolen away with Katie Deere. These were the men who were demanding a high stakes ransom for her safe return.

The least they could do, and which they did, was to make Katie comfortable. She could walk around the hangar and even go outside when accompanied by Tiny. She had all she needed to eat. She could shower twice a day in the abandoned guest quarters of the drug lord's mansion, and she was given a soft bed to sit on throughout the day. She was not treated roughly or threatened, but she was made to know that she was for the time being a captive, and that soon her parents would pay the money to get her back. The trip from Cat Cay to Normans had been scary for her, but since that time she had been more bored than anything else.

On one of her trips outside she asked Tiny, "When can I go?"

"If everything goes right, tonight."

"What if it doesn't go right?"

"You'll be allowed to go as soon as we get our money. It's supposed to be tonight. If your parents cooperate that's how it'll work."

"How much are you getting for me?"

"None of your business. You ask too many questions. Shut up for a while."

Katie turned and kicked Tiny in the leg. He did not flinch; he merely looked down at her in surprise. "Don't do that," he said, as if a pesky mosquito had buzzed his ear. "Be nice or I'll have to tie your hands and feet. Do you want me to tie you up?"

"I want you to let me go. I think you're mean."

"I'm not mean," said Tiny. "Have I been mean to you?"

"You kidnaped me. That's mean!"

"That's just business. You'll be with your parents soon and I want you to tell them that I was nice to you."

"No way!" said Katie. "If you were nice to me you'd let me go."

"And if I release you, where would you go. This island is abandoned. You'd starve to death in a week."

Katie was not thinking in terms of being stranded without food for a week. She considered what Tiny had said. It was true, she could tell her parents that he had been nice to her and that she was never afraid. Except for **the** business at hand, Tiny was not such a bad guy after all.

The last two hours of the ride to Highborne had been thrilling and productive for Cecil. A rogue dolphin, a large bull, hit one of the skirted ballyhoos. Instantly, line screamed off the reel as if without resistance. Gaffer saw that he would have to apply at least a little drag or he would run out of line in a minute. He lightly turned the drag nob on the top of the reel. He handed the rod to Cecil and told him to get busy.

"Take it easy," he said. "Let him run. I'm going to chase him down

147

so he doesn't spool you." Gaffer turned *Bimini Twist* around and headed bow first toward the fleeing game fish. "Walk up to the bow. I'll keep heading toward him and you can reel. I just need you to tell me which direction to steer and whether to slow down or speed up. Don't let the line go slack and let him have as much as he wants."

"Got it," said Cecil. There was no point in trying to fight the fish just yet. It was green, new to the fight, and had a ton of energy. The best thing was to let it wear itself out.

Gaffer called *Lady Liberty* on his VHS and told his father that they were in a fight with a big dolphin and that he would catch up with him when they were finished. Max acknowledged and continued on his route to Highborne Cay.

So for twenty minutes Gaffer steered *Bimini Twist* this way and that, always helping Cecil to maintain a lead against the dolphin. But, at the end of that time, Cecil could see that he was winning the fight. He could raise the rod tip up and then swing it down, taking in line the whole way. Occasionally the fish would take more line out. Cecil's response would be to let him have it, and when it stopped running he would bring in more line. Several times the dolphin jumped high in the air showing its full size and shaking like mad. But by the time they reached the thirty minute mark Cecil was more or less reeling at will. When the fish was within fifty feet of the boat Gaffer called again to his father. "*Lady Liberty*, Dad. Come in."

"What's up?" came the reply.

"I think we've bagged our limit. Cecil has a really nice dolphin almost up to the boat and we need some ice. As soon as I bring it in we're coming along side."

"Can you see us?" asked Max.

148

"I think you're on my horizon. That means you're about five miles out."

Max referred to his radar and could see the green splotch that was *Bimini Twist.* "You got it," said Max. "Five miles."

"All right, I have work to do. Out." He replaced the microphone and reached down for his biggest gaff. He followed Cecil around the boat as the fish took him along the starboard side, around the bow and then down the port side. By now there was no fight left in the huge bull, so Cecil reeled in the last few feet. He held the leader in his hand and brought the fish right up to the boat. Gaffer reached down and gaffed the dolphin just behind its head and in one motion brought it over the gunwale. The fish bucked and flopped and was more than Gaffer could handle. He let it fall to the deck. He then reached into the center console storage compartment and brought out a beach towel. He tossed it over the dolphin and knelt down on it.

"Cecil, open the fish box."

There was desperation in Gaffer's voice. He had never before boated a dolphin this big and he knew that it would be dangerous to let it free to flop around on the deck. It could easily break someone's leg, and it had already gotten blood all over the place. Cecil held the box open while Gaffer lifted the dolphin up and dropped it in. The head and most of the body fit into the box, but two feet of the tail stuck out. The fish flopped around still bucking like crazy but unable to lift Gaffer off the door to the fish box.

"He'll stop flopping in a minute," said Gaffer. "Here, hold this lid down until he dies and I'll get some of this blood off the boat."

Cecil did as he was asked while Gaffer filled a bucket with clean seawater and poured it over the deck. He repeated this procedure twice and then took out a long handled brush to scrub away the blood. It took a full ten minutes before Gaffer was satisfied that he had cleaned up the entire mess. By that time the bull had died. Gaffer went to the helm and throttled up to just above a planing speed, seventeen knots. The boat was pointed at *Lady Liberty* on the horizon, and Gaffer could see it clearly.

"OK, Cecil, take us to the other boat. I'm going to clean this guy or he'll go bad sticking out of the box like that."

"Can we get a picture?" asked Cecil. "That's the biggest fish I ever caught."

"We might just be in luck. Hold it a second. I might have a camera." Gaffer rummaged through the glove box and came up with a disposable instant camera with ten pictures left on it. "We're in luck," he said. He handed Cecil a hand sized lip gaff. "Hold your prize up with this and I'll snap a couple of pictures. This is no world record, but it's still quite an impressive accomplishment for twelve pound test." While Cecil struggled with the fish Gaffer found his scale. Cecil finally raised the fish to a height where its full body was in view. Gaffer had to move back to get the entire body in the shot. The fish was easily five feet long. Gaffer snapped five pictures and put down the camera. He stood along side Cecil and clipped the scale into the dolphin's mouth. He heaved the fish up and took the reading.

"Wow!" Gaffer exclaimed. "Sixty-six pounds. That's huge, by far the biggest dolphin ever caught on *Bimini Twist.*" He set the fish on the deck. "Congratulations." He gave Cecil a high five and then collected his cleaning knife and sharpener. He drew the blade back and forth across the sharpening surface and knelt down over the fish. Cecil returned to the helm and steered toward *Lady Liberty* while Gaffer, as carefully as possible, tore the skin away from the flesh. This was a big fish and it would take a lot of strokes of the cleaning knife before the filets would be free of the bones.

Bimini Twist was approaching the rear of *Lady Liberty* and Gaffer was still kneeling on the deck cutting away the meat. He had filled two three gallon buckets with the filets of the fish and was ready to clean up the mess he had made. He cut the strips of filet into manageable sizes and tossed them into a bucket of clean seawater. When everything had been rinsed at least twice he began filling zip lock bags. It took six one gallon bags to contain all the filets. He looked up and saw that his father was standing only ten feet away on the dive platform of the other boat. He stood up, his joints stiff from kneeling all this time.

"Dad, look at this." He lifted the carcass for his father to see.

"Good lord," exclaimed Max. "What a fish!"

"I weighed it," said Gaffer. "Sixty-six pounds."

"Good lord," repeated Max. He then handed two five pound bags of ice over to Cecil. Gaffer tossed the carcass overboard and placed the bags of filet into the cooler. He poured the two bags of ice over that and was satisfied that the filets would be preserved. While Cecil and Max reattached the towing harness Gaffer poured bucket after bucket of clean seawater over the deck. He then used the long handled brush again to finish cleaning up the mess. Before he knew it, the job was done. The fish was in the cooler and *Bimini Twist* was ship shape. He could now proceed to Highborne Cay feeling like he had an excellent start on the day.

CHAPTER FOURTEEN

Highborne Stopover

By 8:30 AM the Jordans, Diamonds, Max and Gaffer, and the three officers from the Defense Force were all assembled on the rear deck of *Lady Liberty*. This was the best place they could find where everyone could get together and plan strategy. This would be their center of operations. It was roomy, it was comfortable, and it was portable, an ideal situation for what they would be called upon to do later on. *Bimini Twist* had been gassed up, main tank and reserve, and docked in the next slip over.

The first thing Jessica Diamond wanted to do was to give Gaffer a hug for all his efforts. What had started out as a simple delivery of the Diamond family's yacht from Fort Lauderdale to Coral Gables, turned out to be a major big deal where Max had to leave work to join his son for the crossing while the Defense Force was mobilized to take the lead in capturing the kidnappers. Now everyone sat in Highborne Cay, an inconceivable destination only twelve hours earlier, and waited for instructions from a small group of outlaws.

The Diamonds and Jordans remained glued to their cell phone and radio, never knowing which way the call would come. The Defense Force also needed to be immediately available when the call came. That left Max and Gaffer to make a run to the nearby grocery store to stock *Lady Liberty* with enough food to feed everyone for a couple of days. Noting that the groceries Gaffer had bought in the Miami Beach Marina was nice for a quick snack, Max knew that what the boat really needed was just about everything to make a kitchen operate. An hour later he and Gaffer returned to the boat with a golf cart full of grocery bags and $285 lighter. But it was fun for Jessica Diamond to organize her kitchen and prepare the first meal on her new yacht. It kept her busy and took her mind off the problem at hand. Abbey Deere pitched in the best she could. She had difficulty concentrating on the kitchen duties, but it was therapeutic for her also.

The men gathered around the helm with charts of the area spread out on the broad bench seat. Of the entire group, only Max had ever visited the Exumas, and that was so many years ago that his knowledge of it was useless. They looked up and down the island chain on the charts from Highborne to Rum Cay and found no obvious clues as to where the kidnappers might be hiding Katie Deere. However, one important lesson that they learned was that the near shore waters in this area were not all navigable. There were shoals, coral heads, and all manner of other hazards standing in the way of safe boating. Gaffer opened up the chart plotter and called up the chart for this area. The same obstacles that appeared on the paper chart were present on the electronic one. He decided that he would take the paper one with him on *Bimini Twist*. There were no objections.

Cameron Ford placed a call to his home office in Nassau for some direction. The information center on Paradise Island swung into action the minute he called. With their banks of high speed computers, which held information about every crime and every type of criminal activity, and worldwide access to any other type of crime fighting information imaginable, they began setting parameters for where the best likelihood would be for the kidnappers to be holding up. The only half way solid clue they had was that the kidnappers might be three or four black men, and they might be in a small boat that might be grey or white. Not a whole lot of information to go on.

Six locations were given as possibilities. They deduced that the kidnappers would be holding the girl in a location not much further than forty miles away. After all, they had said the switch would be made somewhere near Highborne, and just how far was a reasonable distance? Among the areas that stood out as possibilities were Highborne itself, Hawksbill Cay, Shroud Cay, Normans Cay, Bell Island and Bitter Guana. Unfortunately New Providence Island, the capitol of the Bahamas Islands with a bustling population of 170,000 also fell within the grid, as did Eleuthera which gave the kidnappers a million possibilities for a hide out.

Max and Gaffer could not stand to sit around waiting for a call. They decided to get away from land for a while and do some exploring of their own. Naturally the Diamonds and Jordans would want to stay there and wait for a transmission from the kidnappers. Cameron and his men also stayed nearby as they needed the flexibility to take off either in the boat or the helicopter. Gaffer knew for certain that the Diamonds would not be fishing on this trip so he moved the rest of their bait over to *Bimini Twist*. While their first responsibility was to visit the small nearby islands and report back if they saw anything that might look like a clue, in these fertile waters who knew what opportunities might come up? In addition to the bait, Gaffer brought over some ice and moved the filets from this morning's catch to the refrigerator on *Lady Liberty*. Max made certain they had drinks and a bite to eat for later. When the preparations were complete, they untied from the dock and headed to the south to see what they might find.

Each hour either Gaffer or Max would call in to the team on *Lady*

Liberty. Even as the time passed ten, eleven, noon, there had been no word from Katie's captors. Abbey and Jordan were nearly frantic. They had not seen their daughter in more than twenty-seven hours. They received no information from the Defense Force in Nassau, and both were sporting headaches and upset stomachs from worrying. When one o'clock finally rolled around they decided to cast off and make their own tour of the nearby islands. Cameron went with them while Chet and Cecil stayed behind to be near the chopper.

Since *Bimini Twist* headed south on the inside, choosing to navigate the tricky Yellow Bank, the Diamonds headed south on the outside, in the deeper water of Exuma Sound. They visited cay after cay along the way. They followed every channel marker toward land and stopped in every port they could find. If there was a house on the shore in the distance, they would come in as close as possible, always looking out for a small gray or white boat.

The shallow water of the Yellow Bank made Max very nervous. Even though his depth finder told him that he usually had six feet of water under the transducer in his keel, the clarity of the water was so sharp that it gave the illusion of being much shallower. He stood in the bow watching for obstacles that could be a danger to his boat. Each time he saw a coral rock, and he saw one nearly every few hundred feet, he would have Gaffer steer around it. A few times he was too slow to warn Gaffer and they slid over them. There was still three feet of water under his keel, but that was not comforting as his props needed a minimum of eighteen inches of clearance. But, with the clear water playing tricks on his perception of the depth, Max chose to err on the side of caution. Between the coral heads Max could see that the water was teeming with fish. Most were tropical

155

wrasses, parrotfish, sergeant majors, and yellow tails, as well as triggerfish and queen angels. But that was not all. The barracuda looked young and healthy as did the several good sized groupers he saw. A couple of sharks in the eight hundred pound range also showed up slithering along the bottom. Max kept a rod handy along with a half pound of squid for bait, just in case.

The boat traffic in the area was not heavy and each time one was seen on the horizon Gaffer would check it out with his high powered binoculars. When boats came within 300 yards of him Max would toss a line overboard to make it look like it was a typical day of fishing. By mid afternoon they had made their way down to Halls Pond and decided that this had been a waste of time and headed back toward Highborne. On the outside of the island chain, a mile offshore in the Exuma Sound, the group on board *Lady Liberty* was coming to the same conclusion. *Bimini Twist's* radio sparked to life.

"*Bimini Twist, Lady Liberty*. Come in."

Gaffer keyed the mike, "*Bimini Twist.*"

"*Bimini Twist*, where are you?"

"We're just turning around to head back. We're at Halls Pond. Where are you?"

"Staniel," came the reply.

"All the way down there," said Gaffer. "See anything?"

"Not yet."

"Have they called?"

"Not yet."

Max picked up the handset. "Listen, Jeremy, in about four hours we're going to be seeing the sun start setting. We don't know this area that well and we don't want to have to deal with the darkness. We're going to head back at a slow pace and check things out one more time. We want to try to make it into Highborne well before sunset."

"That sounds smart," said Jeremy. "I think we'll turn back too. See you in Highborne."

"OK," replied Max. "*Bimini Twist,* out."

A half hour after that transmission, while *Bimini Twist* was cruising slowly by Hawksbill Cay, a boat passed them. Max and Gaffer had been looking to the north and east, so when the boat passed them from the south, headed north, they were startled. No more than fifty yards on their stern was a boat that fit the description of the one that had been identified at Cat Cay. It was a twenty-seven foot walk around, white hull, single engine. Not an exact match to the one described by the housekeeper at Cat, but the closest thing they had seen all day. It was driven by a single black man. He was alone, moving about as fast as that boat could go, headed toward Normans Cay. Max let the boat pass and get a hundred yards ahead before calling to the Viking.

"*Lady Liberty, Bimini Twist.* Come in *Lady Liberty.*"

"Go Max."

"Jeremy, I just saw the first possible sign of something. A boat vaguely fitting the description of the one we're looking for just passed me. There was one man, looked like a Bahamian native."

On board *Lady Liberty,* Cameron picked up the mike. "Where Max? Where are you and where did he go?"

Max recognized Cameron's voice. "Yeah, Cameron. I'm near Hawksbill right now. I'd say the boat was headed toward Highborne or possibly Normans."

Cameron was well familiar with Normans Cay and its reputation for harboring smugglers in the early days of the drug trade. He had never been there but he could imagine the kidnappers hiding out there. It would have made sense.

"Max, did you go by Normans on your way down the chain?"

"Yeah, we went in. We didn't see any boats. The dock is all broken down. We could see some buildings in the distance but no boats and no people, so we kept on going."

"Can you still see that boat?"

"Oh yeah," said Max. "He's now about a mile and a half in front of us."

"Can you shadow him from that distance. I don't want you to catch up to him but I'd like to know where he goes."

"I'll try," said Max.

"OK, but if he goes into port, you stay offshore. Just find out what port he goes into and call us."

"Ten-four," came the reply. Max hung up the handset and closed the radio compartment door. "You heard him, Gaffer. Let's go."

Gaffer pushed the throttles to the wall until *Bimini Twist* was on a plane and cruising at thirty knots. There was a chop of about two feet and that was too much speed to be comfortable. He pulled back a little and found that twenty-four was a much more comfortable speed, and was just about right to keep the same interval with the boat they were following. They kept this pace for twenty-five minutes before the boat ahead of them made a wide turn to the east and headed into Normans Cay. As soon as there was no mistaking the boat's destination Gaffer pulled back on the throttles and sat still at idle. He lifted the handset and called Cameron.

"*Lady Liberty, Bimini Twist.* Over."

"Go ahead Gaffer." It was Cameron's voice.

"OK, the boat went into Normans Cay. We're drifting about four miles offshore. What do you want us to do?"

"Stay right there, Gaffer," said Cameron. "Mr. Deere is talking on the cell phone I'll call you back in five."

"Ten-four, *Bimini Twist* standing by."

Gaffer baited a 4/0 hook with a strip of squid and tossed it overboard. Max did the same. While they waited for something, anything to happen, Jordan Deere was listening to the sweet voice of his little girl. After allowing fifteen seconds for the girl to tell her father that she loved him and had not been harmed, Pee Wee Wolfe roughly took the phone away from her came back on the line.

"OK, Mr. Deere. You know that your daughter is safe and well. All we want to do is return her to you and collect our money. Are you in agreement with that?"

"Yes, yes. That's all I want."

"We will make the switch tonight. You have not contacted the police, have you? I told you not to call them."

"I didn't," lied Jordan Deere. In truth, he had not contacted them, they had contacted him. But he was in the middle of it now. If he thought he could get his daughter back any sooner by sending the Defense Force home, he would have done it. His focus was entirely on his daughter's safety. "Tell me what I must do. I have your money."

"I will send someone for the money and then I will set your daughter free."

Cameron was listening in to the conversation. He shook his head

159

vehemently. He mouthed, "No, you want to see the girl when you turn the money over."

Jordan Deere stammered, "No, Sir. I want to see my daughter when I turn over the money."

Pee Wee said, "This is my show, not yours. I'll call you in a few hours. I'll tell you where to go and when. No cops. Come alone."

The connection was broken. Jordan turned to Cameron. "What do I do now? He said no cops."

"He doesn't know that we're here. And there's no reason for him to find out either. I'm going to ask you again to calm down and let us do our job. Your job right now is to comfort your wife. "

"We're just so nervous," said Abbey Deere. "We'd do anything to have our girl back safely."

"I know," said Cameron. "But we're not only going to get your daughter back safely, we're also going to capture the kidnappers so that no other family has to go through what you're going through now. You want that, don't you?"

Reluctantly Mr. and Mrs. Deere agreed. Cameron picked up the VHS radio mike. "*Bimini Twist, Lady Liberty.* Over.

Max answered. "*Bimini Twist.*"

"We just received the call. We're coming to your location. It'll take about an hour."

"OK, see you then," replied Max, as he turned and attended to his fishing rod.

Cameron next called to his men back at Highborne. Cecil was quick to pick up his cell phone. "Cecil, the call came from the kidnappers. They confirmed that the swap will be tonight. Max saw a boat that matches the description of the boat in Cat Cay. He's sitting offshore Normans Cay. We're going there now to meet up with him."

"What are our orders?" asked Cecil.

"Have the helicopter pilot bring you to *Bimini Twist*. You can be there in a few minutes. Wait there for us."

"Do you have the coordinates?"

"Hold on, I'll pick them up on the radar." Cameron was off the air for **three** minutes while he located *Bimini Twist* on the radar screen, and then acquired the GPS coordinates. He came back on the radio and read them to Cecil who put them in his handheld GPS immediately.

"OK, good," said Cecil. "I picked up a detailed map of the area, each of the islands and a close up of the water between here and Staniel. What else do you want us to do before we head over?"

"Make several copies of the detail on Normans. Then get going," said Cameron. "I'm calling Nassau and we're heading toward Normans. We'll all be together within an hour and we'll put our entire strategy together at that time."

Cecil clicked off his radio and headed up the narrow rubble road where he knew there was a copy machine in the customs office. In another ten minutes he and Chet Cristie were piling into the helicopter. The chopper lifted off and flew at only twenty feet above the surface of the water so as not to be noticed in case the kidnappers were looking seaward. In five minutes *Bimini Twist* was in view, and two minutes after that Cecil and Chet were repelling on long ropes out the open door and down to the deck of the boat. The helicopter pilot showed exceptional skill as he held the aircraft perfectly still and Chet and Cecil landed on their feet on the deck of the boat. Max and Gaffer stood with their mouths agape as they watched these professional lawmen in action. The chopper took off toward Highborne again traveling low to the surface of the water. It was an exciting, adrenaline-filled few minutes for the father and son, and the two Defense Force officers.

FIFTEEN

"Tiny" Regan

"Please don't start acting up now. I don't want to have to spank you. Your parents are coming to get you in a few hours, so behave." Tiny knew he had a bored, rambunctious little girl on his hands, and he was winded from having to chase her around the airstrip. She had bolted for the hangar door and took off down the tarmac. The only thing slowing her down was the fact that she was running barefooted. That slowed her sufficiently for Tiny to be able to catch her. He had been gentle with her all along and it did not surprise her that he merely walked back along side her with his hand resting on her shoulder. Katie would have been shocked had he acted any other way. In her quiet moments she thought that if a person had to be kidnaped, they should ask for Tiny to be their jailer.

As they walked through the wide hangar door, Axle was standing just inside waiting for them. His face was contorted in a mask of fury. "What do you think you're doing?" he screamed at the little girl. "I ought to . . ."

He did not finish his sentence. He stormed at her with his hand raised to give her a solid slap across her little face. Tiny stepped between them and caught the arm in full swing.

"That's enough," he said. "You don't need to be touching that girl. She just ran out for some exercise. She's back and I have her under control."

Katie hid behind the big man to keep out of the reach of the angry attacker. But Axle was not done venting. He shoved Tiny back, hoping to get around him at the girl. All of Tiny's paternal instincts came out, as he quickly grasped the attacking man by the throat with his left hand while he landed a solid punch into Axle's gut with his right hand. Axle hit the ground and did not get up again. Tiny knelt down with the full weight of his knee on Axle's chest. "If I have to tell you again to leave that girl alone, you'll be sorry. Now keep your hands off of her."

Tiny stood up and carried Katie to the back of the hangar and placed her on her bed. "Are you all right?" he asked.

Katie began to cry. "I just want to be with my parents," she said with tears streaming down her face. "And I hate Axle. He's mean and I hate him."

Tiny smiled at the little girl and sympathized with her. He answered, "You're not alone. Axle doesn't have many friends. I don't like him much either."

"Then why won't you let me go?" Katie begged.

"You'll be with your parents in a few hours. We're arranging the transfer now and you'll be with them probably within six hours. How about we have something to eat or play some cards or something to pass the time."

"I just want my parents," said Katie petulantly. "I don't want your stupid food or your stupid cards. And you're stupid too."

"Nice talk," said Tiny. "Don't forget, I'm the guy who's keeping Axle from smacking you. Would you like me to let him at you?"

"You wouldn't dare," said the little girl. "I'll bet you have kids and are thinking, what if that were my daughter or son, aren't you?"

"I don't have kids, or a wife, or a girl friend,"

Katie answered, "Because you're too mean to have anybody love you."

Tiny was shocked and hurt. He stood and began walking away.

By now Axle had recovered and was walking toward where Katie was sitting on the bed. As he passed Tiny he scowled at him but said nothing, and kept walking toward the little girl. Katie screamed, thinking that Axle was really going to smack her. And he was.

Katie jumped down from the bed and ran as fast as she could to get away from the angry Axle. He broke into a run to catch her, but seeing this, Tiny also broke into a run to catch them both. Katie looked back to see that Axle was between her and Tiny. She was terrified for what he might do to her if he caught her. The only hope was to maneuver around and place Tiny between her and Axle. But just as she was about to make a quick left turn, she slipped on a sandy spot and went skidding across the floor. Axle slowed and stood over her, just long enough for Tiny to catch up. Axle lifted the girl roughly and drew his hand back to slap her across her face. He was a split second too late as Tiny's giant fist slammed into the side of his head knocking him out cold. Axle crumbled to the floor in a heap.

Katie was badly shaken. She had scrapes on her face, shoulder and leg, and tears streamed down her face through dirt and small patches of abraised skin. Tiny lifted her and held her as she hugged his neck and cried on his shoulder. He returned her to her bed and sat her down gently.

"Now why do you want to make all this trouble?" he asked. "Look what you caused. You're all skinned up and bleeding, and poor Mr. Axle is going to madder than ever when he wakes up."

"I hate him," said Katie. "He's the meanest man I ever saw."

"I admit that he's not very nice. That's a good reason for you to not make him mad. He's the one who's supposed to give you back to your mother and father."

"Can't you do it?" pleaded Katie.

"Why can't you just leave things alone. Keep out of it and you can still get to be with your parents. But if you make Mr. Axle mad again, well I'll just say, he's got a gun."

"That doesn't scare me," said Katie. "He's not going to shoot me. He wouldn't do that."

"Yeah," agreed Tiny. "But that wouldn't keep him from shooting me."

"No," screamed Katie. She jumped into Tiny's arms and hugged his neck. "He can't do that," she cried.

"Then you better behave or we'll both be in trouble."

Katie peered over to where Axle lay on the deck out cold. "Why don't we just tie him up?"

"Don't worry. I can handle him, but you have to behave."

Katie relaxed. Tiny let her down and took her by the hand over to where the groceries were stored. He reached into a cooler and pulled out a can of Coke and gave it to the girl. She opened it and took a sip. She offered it to Tiny but he declined.

"Look, Sweetie," said Tiny. "You're going to see your parents soon. You need to clean up and make yourself look pretty. You want to look good for your parents, don't you?"

Tiny began to lead Katie toward the door and over to the shower when Stingray Brown came around the corner and nearly crashed into him.

"What's up?" asked Stingray.

"I'm taking the girl to let her clean up. Axle chased her around the hangar and she fell and skinned herself up."

Stingray looked over at where Axle was out cold on the floor. He gasped. "What happened to him?"

Tiny shuffled around where he stood. "The truth is, he was out of control with the girl. He chased her and threatened to smack her. I restrained him once, but he came at her again. I had to get rough with him."

Stingray moved over to where Axle lay on the floor. He looked up at Tiny. "Are you crazy? He's out cold."

"He made me do it. We might be kidnappers, but there's no reason to take it out on the girl. Axle was being a bully and I had to stop him. I had to stop him twice. The girl is no trouble, she's just a little girl."

Stingray did not argue with Tiny. He knew of Axle's temper and it came as no surprise that he had to be restrained. He leaned over the unconscious man and shook him. Axle began to stir. He rolled over on his back and groaned. His eyes opened but he did not try to get up. His head was splitting. Tiny chose to not wait around to hear what Axle had to say about this turn of events. He continued on with Katie to the shower room.

When Katie and Tiny returned to the hangar after twenty minutes, Axle was sitting on a chair speaking with Stingray. He said nothing to Tiny but gave him a deadly scowl. Tiny walked over to Axle and got right up in his face.

"If you're going to say something to me, say it now."

With a look of disgust on his face Axle said, "I got nothin' to say."

"Then that's the end of it. We finish this job and I'm out of here.

You're a loser and a totally useless bum," said Tiny. "I don't want to see you again and you stay away from me."

"That's fine. We grab our money and were done." After a moment he said, "And you keep that little brat away from me."

Tiny's patience was worn out. "Just shut up about the girl. She's no problem of yours. You stay away from her and you'll have no problem with me. You go near her again and I'll make you sorrier than you've ever been in your life."

Axle blanched at the threat. He knew that Tiny could tear him apart if he wanted to. He said nothing.

SIXTEEN

Assault on Norman's Cay

Lady Liberty idled up to where *Bimini Twist* sat at anchor. Cameron was on one side of the bow and Jordan was on the other, both looking out for coral heads that might be a danger to the underside of the yacht. Jeremy Diamond was extremely nervous looking down and seeing the bottom through the clearest water in this part of the planet. It looked so close. Max had anchored in twelve feet of water knowing that the larger boat had a deeper draft. Still, Jeremy could not stop the small beads of sweat from forming on his brow. He picked up the VHS and called across to Max.

"There's not enough water here to be safe. I'd like to move a couple of miles further offshore."

"OK," Max called back. "We also need to get out of view of the island. We wouldn't want to be seen here. You never know what they might think is going on if they happen to see us."

Cameron came back on the radio. "I agree. Let's go."

"I'll follow you," responded Max. He cranked his engines to life as Chet pulled the anchor. In less than five minutes they were planing at twenty knots, headed due west. Ten minutes after that, Normans Cay was a speck on the distant horizon. *Bimini Twist* came along side *Lady Liberty*. Jeremy Diamond looked relieved that he now had twenty feet of water under his keel.

In the late afternoon, the breeze had died down and the sea was calm. *Lady Liberty's* anchor splashed into the sea and gripped the sandy bottom. *Bimini Twist* idled around to the yacht's stern and Jordan Deere stood in the cockpit ready to catch a line from Cecil Hunter. Then the passengers on board *Bimini Twist* climbed over to *Lady Liberty* to discuss the current situation and strategy for the balance of the day. Cameron was officially in charge of any plans they made.

"Because we know that the exchange will be made after dark, Cecil and Chet are going to go in just after sunset and snoop around. Max, you bring them to within three hundred yards of shore and they can swim the rest of the way."

Chet made a small frown. "Why does it have to be three hundred yards, why can't it be three hundred feet?" Max stepped in to help.

"It doesn't have to be even that far. I've been examining the map of the island and if getting to the abandoned compound is what you want to do, I can drop them off on the other side of the point where there's a sandy beach and they won't have to swim at all."

"How long of a walk will it be from the beach to the compound?" asked Cameron.

Max referred to the map. "Two inches on the map," he replied.

Cameron's head snapped up. He looked quizzically at Max. "I was just kidding. Lighten up." Cameron shook his head but he did give a small chuckle. Chet smiled broadly but restrained himself from laughing out loud.

"Can you possibly be serious?" asked Cameron.

"OK, OK. So it's no time to be funny. But to answer the question, there's no scale on the map. But cross referencing the map to the nautical chart, it looks like it might be a half mile to the end of the runway and another mile and a half after that."

Cameron looked at Chet and Cecil. "You guys want to walk two miles or swim a hundred yards?"

"It's not what I'd rather do, but what makes the most sense," said Cecil. "If they're guarding the place at all it's going to be from the water side. I don't think they'll be expecting an approach from the land. We should go the way Max suggested. We can jog the two miles in fifteen minutes. Max can let us off on the beach side and pick us up on the marina side. I don't mind swimming out of there, but I hate showing up wet, getting my weapons wet, and not being able to move around as well in soaking clothes. All-in-all, I think we ought to approach across the runway."

"I'm with you," said Chet.

"Ok, I want you each to have a hand held VHS radio. Take some emergency flairs, whatever weapons you want. You'll go ashore at eighteen thirty hours. While we wait I want you to get fed and prepare your weapons, ammunition and gear." Cameron was finished with the instructions for his men. He picked up his cell phone and called Virgil Price in Nassau. It was time to report in once again.

Cameron told Virgil everything that had transpired up until this time. He told him that the greatest likelihood would be for the kidnappers to be on Normans Cay, and he told him about the plans to have Cecil and Chet recon the area. Virgil authorized the action.

"I'm going to dispatch two helicopters to your area," said Virgil. "We'll reinforce you with sixteen men. Four will be on each of the boats, and four will remain on each of the choppers. Between the two boats and the two helicopters, the kidnappers will not stand a chance. The most important thing will be the safe return of the little girl." Virgil was as concerned as a caring human being as he was as a law enforcement officer. As an afterthought he asked, "How are the parents holding up?"

"Not well," responded Cameron. "They're quite upset."

"Well, tell them that I guarantee that everything will be all right."

"I'll tell them that," said Cameron. "By the way, I just want to be certain you know that Max and Gaffer are helping out. I hope you don't mind. You know, it's that question about using civilians on our operations."

"Is Max OK with it?" asked Virgil.

"You know Max and Gaffer; whatever it takes."

"I just don't want to wear out our welcome with them, they've already done so much."

"Don't worry about it, Chief. You'll never hear them complain. The only thing is Max is a little worried about Gaffer missing three days of school just before the Christmas break. I think he had some finals."

"Oh," said Virgil, "that's not good."

"Perhaps a note from the Superintendent of the Royal Bahamas Defense Force to his principal will make a difference."

It sounded absurd and Virgil laughed. "Who'd believe it?"

Cameron was smiling. "Maybe if you use some of that pretty, official-looking stationery."

Now Virgil really laughed. "I'll do whatever I have to. Tell the little rascal not to worry."

"No, Boss. Gaffer is definitely not worried. It's his father who's worried."

"OK, tell him I'll give him a note."

"I'll tell him that."

"I've got to jump off. Give your coordinates to my assistant and the choppers will be there in less than an hour." Virgil handed the phone to the young Defense Force officer and instructed her to take down the information Cameron gave her. He went about his business while a special detachment of troops made preparations for the short flight to offshore Normans Cay.

While they waited for the choppers to arrive, Max and Gaffer cleaned up the decks on *Bimini Twist.* They would be cruising with Chet and Cecil and four other Defense Force operatives. There would be eight men on board all together, six of whom would be loaded with gear. They would need all the sitting room they could manage. Meanwhile, on *Lady Liberty* arrangements were being made to accept their new guests on board.

As the sun met the sea on the western horizon, Chet and Cecil began making preparations for the reconnaissance mission. They changed out of their civilian attire and donned their camouflage stealth gear. They spread camouflage grease their faces and armed themselves to the teeth. Both men preferred the 1911 Colt forty-five caliber semi-automatic pistol. Each man wore two. They filled their belts and pockets with an array of survival gear for an assault on a hostage position, including their razor sharp k-bars, high intensity illumination flares, flash/bang grenades, night vision goggles, hand held GPS, and high tech radio communications equipment. Gaffer looked at them and tried to take in all the unfamiliar gear. His friends, Cecil and Chet, had been transformed into fighting machines. They looked truly fierce and Gaffer could not hide his awe.

Each of the boat crews were just finishing their clean up when the sounds of helicopters could be heard, first faintly in the distance, and then louder and louder until they reached the area of the boats. The first chopper hovered above *Bimini Twist* as the pilot established communications with Cameron. He instructed the team captain to have the first four officers repel down to *Bimini Twist's* deck. The second helicopter held back, hovering twenty feet off the surface of the water.

As the men slid down their ropes to *Bimini Twist*, Gaffer stood with his mouth agape. These guys did it like it was something they did everyday. They landed hard on the surface of the boat and let go of the ropes. These men were the elite of the Defense Force, as were Chet and Cecil, and it was a happy reunion for the six operatives. Cecil took command of this team. He instructed Gaffer to untie from *Lady Liberty* and for Max to start the engines.

It was dusk, only twenty minutes until pitch dark. Cecil gave Max the order to take off. He had hoped to use the last few moments of daylight to navigate to the beach on the opposite side of Normans Cay. In the best of circumstances Max hated to drive his boat at night. This was much worse, beginning to get dark, no moon to provide even a hint of light, unfamiliar and very dangerous water. And to make things worse he could not use his navigation lights as this was a stealth mission. There were ten miles between this location and the beach on the opposite side of Normans Cay. Max took into consideration that he was part of a team that was trying to rescue a helpless little girl. With that thought in mind he stopped worrying about the boat, and the props, and any other consideration for the welfare of his boat. The stakes were much higher than that.

Bimini Twist moved through the water at twenty knots. Max was at the helm while Gaffer and Cecil huddled on the deck of the cockpit examining a chart of the waters surrounding Normans Cay, illuminated by a small penlight. The boat's current heading of 165 degrees would take them past the southern point through water that never became shallower than four feet at mean low water. Several shoal areas would need to be avoided as well as an area of coral heads just under the surface. According to Cecil's calculations at their current speed they were about fifteen minutes from the dangerous area. Gaffer joined his father on the leaning post at the helm.

"This is going to be very tricky in a few minutes," Gaffer warned him. "The water on the way to the point in not good."

Max asked, "Is the bad area in view of the marina on the island?"

"Let me look," answered Gaffer. He knew what his father was thinking. It was everyone's theory that the kidnappers were somewhere near the small basin that they had referred to as the marina. Perhaps there was a house or a building or some place where the kidnappers could hide out until the exchange was made. If they were out of sight of this basin when they entered the treacherous, coral-laced water, then it would cause no harm to shine a light into the water to help them avoid a meeting of the props with the coral heads.

Cecil agreed that if the boat were out of sight of the marina that the use of the light would be a good idea. He and Gaffer poured over the chart again, drawing lines this way and that, studying the best route through. The good news was that there was no possible way to see *Bimini Twist* from anywhere near the marina. It was decided that they would chance it with the lights.

Ten minutes later Gaffer tapped his father on the shoulder. "This is it," he said. "Slow down. We've got a couple of miles of bad water."

175

Max pulled back on the throttles and brought the boat to eight knots. This proved to be a bad speed as the boat could not plane at that speed and the props tended to be much deeper in the water with the stern of the boat down and the bow up. He would have to either speed up to plane, or slow down to near idle. While idle speed would be the safest choice, it would take them too long to get where they were going. He decided to get up on a plane. He would have to be going fifteen knots to do that. It would be disastrous for the boat if they hit something at that speed, but it was also fast enough so that the boat needed less water to cruise.

Gaffer lay on the bow with his light fixed on the water ahead of him. He strained his eyes to see into the water ahead of the boat. But they were going too fast. He snapped off the light and made his way back to the helm. "This won't work," he told his father. "At this speed before I could warn you, you would have already run something over."

"Then there's only one thing to do," said Max. He pushed the throttles forward and brought the boat to twenty-eight knots. "At this speed we really only need about a foot of water." For an additional measure of safety he pressed the tilt button for the engines. The props tilted up about four more inches and the bow of the boat came further out of the water. "This is probably our best angle," he said. "But if we hit something, it won't be good."

To try to encourage him Cecil said flippantly, "Then I suggest you don't hit anything."

Max's breath was coming is short bursts. His eyes had adjusted to the darkness and from time to time he could see large dark objects pass under the boat. He did not know if they were coral heads, grass patches, shoal areas, or what. He just kept going, nervous, jittery, and worried to death. It would not be so bad if a prop touched bottom. They could bend or break, but they were easily replaced. But if they ran hard aground, not only would that destroy the boat, but his passengers could be badly injured by the sudden, jarring stop.

Those dark objects passing under the hull were making Max very nervous. He gritted his teeth against the crunch that he was certain would come. Gaffer offered him water, or something else to take his mind off the current problem. But nothing calmed him. This was too scary. Cecil also saw Max's nervousness but he decided to let the man alone with his thoughts and leave the rest up to fate.

Gaffer joined Cecil for another look at the chart spread out on the deck. Gaffer ran his finger along an imaginary line from where they began their trek across the banks to where he thought they could be five minutes later. It appeared that in another two or three minutes they would be back in the good water and only two miles from the beach where they were to let off the men. He returned to the helm and told his father the news. Max seemed visibly to relax. In a less than steady voice all he said was, "I hate driving at night."

Once out of the shoal area Max asked Gaffer to take over the helm while he and Cecil made one more check of the chart together. Each man wanted to be certain they understood where the rendezvous spot would be when the men returned from the reconnaissance mission. They agreed that one way or another the men would end up moving through the marina but, because of the uncertainty of what they might find on the island, they had to recommend against Max bringing *Bimini Twist* too close to shore. They selected a spot a quarter mile offshore and to the south of the marina entrance for the boat to wait to rendezvous with the team. Cecil and his men would try to be there within an hour. Max, barring a meeting of his props with the sea bottom, would be there within thirty minutes and would drop anchor to wait for him. According to the chart the depth at this location at low tide, which unfortunately it was now, was two to three feet with rock outcrops everywhere.

As *Bimini Twist* idled at a snails pace into the beach, Gaffer shined his flashlight into the water. This was a perfect location for what they were doing. The bottom was pure sand and they would be able to bring the boat all the way up to the beach. As they did that and the bow touched land, the men all piled off the boat. As they jumped off the bow, Gaffer considered for a minute what the boots of the six men were doing to the gel-coat finish. It was just a momentary, natural reaction that he dismissed the instant all six men were safely ashore. The last man off the boat turned and shoved *Bimini Twist* back away from the beach. Max hit reverse with both engines for just long enough to put about a twenty-five foot distance between himself and the shore. From that distance he and Gaffer huddled on the deck to chart their best route to the rendezvous location.

SEVENTEEN

Amphibious Assault

As soon as the men hit the beach they ran up the shallow embankment and disappeared in the darkness. Within a few minutes they had acquired the landing strip and began at a trot toward the compound. With their night vision goggles they could see the buildings in the far distance. They planned to move at double time to a point two hundred yards from the nearest building and then move slowly and quietly the rest of the way into the compound. It took seventeen minutes for them to arrive at that point. They moved over to the side of the runway and crouched in the overgrown weeds. It would have been impossible to see them from more than twenty feet away.

Cecil huddled with his men. They had reached the point where contact with the kidnappers was a possibility. It was time to arm themselves. Cecil carried in his hands his forty-five and high powered flashlight. Each of the other men carried their sidearms and one or another type of weapon, including k-bars, stun guns, and pepper sprays. Chet and Cecil crawled out onto the runway and looked toward the compound. Through night vision goggles they could easily tell that three of the buildings, including the hangar, the main house and a tool shed were showing lights. There were no people to be seen. They crawled back into the weeds and Cecil raised Cameron on his headset radio.

"Cameron, Cecil. Radio check."

Cameron's voice came across immediately. "Loud and clear."

"Any word from the kidnappers yet?"

"Not yet," said Cameron. "Have you found anything?"

"It looks active," said Cecil. "I see lights."

"Proceed cautiously and report back every fifteen minutes."

"Ten-four."

Cecil instructed his men. "We're going to advance in teams of two, leapfrogging to within twenty yards of the small shed. We'll find cover and then Chet and I will recon the shed. We'll decide what to do next based upon what we see or hear when we get there. Any questions?" There were no questions.

The men began advancing in twos. It took only a minute for all three teams to cover a hundred yards. Now it was time to move even more cautiously. Again Cecil looked around. Still no sign of people. He stationed his men under the protection of the rusty hulk of an abandoned bulldozer. He and Cecil took off the goggles and continued in the crouch position up to the side wall of the maintenance shed. Cecil signed to Chet to stay where he was as he crawled up to the door of the shed and peeked his head around the doorjamb. It was a simple building with a single room twenty feet by ten feet. There was nothing in it but some discarded paint cans, landscape tools, and sand bags. There was no one there so Cecil quickly entered the building, looked around, and exited. He rejoined Chet and sat in the cover of the building wall. They sat quietly and listened for sounds.

Max had the luxury of being able to move to the rendezvous point at slower than idle speed. He knew he was outside the view of anyone on shore so he could move around the point with Gaffer holding his light in the water ahead of where they were going. Any time he saw something he did not like he would call it back to his father who could easily steer around or back off. At this rate it would take an hour to get to the rendezvous point but he had no reason to hurry and took comfort in moving at the slower, safer speed. He decided to check in.

"*Lady Liberty*, this is *Bimini Twist*. Come in," said Max.

"Go ahead Max," said Jeremy Diamond.

"Any word yet?"

"Still waiting. How are you doing?"

"We dropped our cargo on the beach and we're making our way carefully to the rendezvous point. Have you heard from Cecil?"

"We just did," replied Jeremy. "They're doing well, no news yet. If we hear anything I'll call you."

"OK," said Max. "*Bimini Twist*, out."

They continued on their way carefully plying the water, constantly looking for hazards. It was a slow go but necessary if they were to avoid a catastrophe.

EIGHTEEN

Shallows at Night

At 7:45 PM the radio on board *Lady Liberty* came to life with the gruff sound of Axle Wolfe's voice. Jordan Deere nearly jumped out of his skin. His nerves were frayed and his anticipation level was off the charts. Axle gave him a set of coordinates twelve miles to the west of Highborne Cay that he wanted to use as a rendezvous point in exactly three hours. He allowed Jordan to speak with his daughter for fifteen seconds and then yanked the microphone away. "If you want to see your daughter again, you'll leave the police out of this."

"I understand, no police. When will I get my daughter back?"

"The instant the money changes hands and my courier is safely away from the pick-up location, he'll radio back to me and I'll give you the location of where to pick her up." Axle failed to mention the part about himself being the courier. The Deeres knew no different and that is the way Axle wanted it.

"Why should I trust you?" asked Jordan.

"Because you have no other choice." Axle said this and turned off the radio.

Were it not for the assistance he was receiving from the Diamonds, the Carsons, and the Defense Force, it would be a hopeless dilemma. But he took comfort in knowing that there were people helping him, and he felt certain that with this assistance he would soon have his daughter back.

Bimini Twist sat at anchor at its predesignated rendezvous location. There was nothing to do but wait. After sitting still for ten minutes Gaffer and Max were both already bored. Gaffer shone his flashlight into the water and saw that the area was teeming with fish. Mostly what he saw was the colorful reef fish that continued to swim around the rocks and coral heads twenty-four hours a day, looking for food and fighting for survival. Gaffer tied a small 2/0 hook onto the leader line of one of the rods. He baited it with an inch square piece of squid and placed a small split lead on the line. He dropped the hook into the water under the boat and waited. He did not expect much, but he was OK with the idea of hooking some of the small reef fish for fun, and then throwing them back. Max lay down in the bow and placed a cushion under his head. They might be here for a while so he attempted to fight boredom by getting some sleep.

Immediately following the call to *Lady Liberty*, the kidnappers brought their hostage out to the marina. They cranked up the boat's engine, untied the lines and idled out of the basin. Axle had been stewing for hours over the incident with Tiny earlier in the day. He had given some thought to throwing him overboard when they got offshore, but a tussle with the big man might end up with the wrong person in the water. He used a lot of negative energy contemplating revenge.

The radios on *Bimini Twist* and the one Cecil was carrying came to life. It was Cameron with an update. "The kidnappers just called. They want to make the exchange in three hours. What is your situation?"

Max answered first. "*Bimini Twist*. We're just around the sandbar from the rendezvous point."

Cecil's radio squawked back, "We're in the building complex, about

183

to search the main house. After that we will search the airplane hangar, and then we'll be making our way to the rendezvous point."

"How soon can you be finished you search?" asked Cameron.

"I need about twenty minutes."

"Make it ten and then high tail it to the rendezvous point. Max, are you listening?"

"I'm here."

"Proceed to the rendezvous point and pick up my men. If they don't find anything more on the island, I'll need you on the water."

As Max was having this conversation, Gaffer pulled the anchor and stowed it. Max hit the ignitions and turned the boat toward the tip of the island. He carefully checked his charts and then called Cecil.

"Cecil, *Bimini Twist.*"

By now Cecil had split his team into two groups, one was entering the abandoned house, the other was approaching the hangar. He responded to the call. "Go ahead Max."

"Cecil, if the island is secure, I want to change the rendezvous point."

"Where to, Max?"

"If the kidnappers are on the run, if they have already left the island, I'll pick you up in the marina. I can run two miles offshore in the water I'm in now, head two miles to the north and then follow the channel in. I can go at a normal speed and be there in twenty minutes. If I go to the original pick-up point, it'll take me an extra forty minutes."

Cecil responded, "Start heading out with that plan. I'll sent two of my men down to the marina to see if the boat is still there. If it has left, then proceed as you just described."

"Ten-four," came the response from *Bimini Twist*. Max moved west at a slow pace, not more than eight knots. He referred to the chart again. He had three feet of water under the keel and would be OK if no coral outcropping appeared. He showed Gaffer what he saw on the chart. They agreed that to be on a plane, needing only a foot to a foot and a half, of water was preferable to idling where they would need two and a half feet to clear the props. Max sped up to twenty knots, the boat planed, he tilted the engines up as far as he dared and steered west by north west. In five minutes he was in eight feet of water and ready to make his swing to the north to pick up the line to the channel marking the entrance to the marina.

By the time Max had made it into the deeper water, Cecil's men had made it to the marina. The call came back that the marina had no boats in it. Cecil called that information in to *Bimini Twist* and to *Lady Liberty*. "The kidnappers are on the move. They have left the island." Cecil then collected the rest of his men and led them to the marina to wait for their pick-up.

The kidnappers had cleared the same channel that Max and Gaffer were going to use only ten minutes earlier. They were now traveling offshore and headed northeast. While they were only four miles to the north of *Bimini Twist's* location, they were running without lights and could not be seen. Cameron watched closely on the radar screen. He saw the kidnappers' boat on the move and he saw *Bimini Twist* not far behind it. He called on his radio, "Max, they're just four miles ahead of you. Can you see them?"

Max strained his eyes as did Gaffer. He called back, "I can barely see my bow, it's so dark out here. What do you want me to do?"

"Continue on your course to pick up the team on the island. Take your time and be careful. We've come this far and it would be a shame for someone to get hurt or have hull damage now. Call me when you have the team."

"Consider it done," came the reply.

By now *Bimini Twist* was even with the entrance marker to the channel. Max turned to the east. At twenty knots his depth finder read the bottom perfectly. He still had ten feet of water under his keel, so he gunned the motor to twenty-six knots. In no more that three minutes he could see the horizon of the island which told him he was now only two miles offshore. As he watched the water become shallower on his depth finder, he slowed. He picked up the radio and called to Cecil. "I'll be there in five minutes," he said.

Cecil replied, "Max, turn on your nav lights so I can see you."

Max hit the switch. The red and green lights on his bow and the white light above his T-top came to life.

"I've got you," he heard Cecil say. Then Cecil prepared his men to board *Bimini Twist*. In spite of the darkness, Max could now see the entrance to the marina clearly. He slowed to make his approach. Again he checked his depth. What was this? The red line indicating bottom had disappeared into the top of the recorder. He pulled the throttles back to neutral. What had happened became immediately obvious. He had lost the channel and was now on the bank. As the boat came to a stop he looked down and saw that perhaps one to two feet of water separated his underside from the bottom. He looked back and could just barely see that he had been kicking up the bottom and leaving a trail of sandy soup behind the boat. He stopped the boat and turned off the engines as he did not want to draw sand into the intakes. He picked up his radio and called Cecil.

"Do you still see me?"

"What's up?" asked Cecil.

"I lost the channel. I'm on the bank but I'm afloat. Gaffer and I will have to walk the boat back to the channel. I think it's about two hundred feet behind us."

"You're not that far from my location. Do you want us to come out and help? We can swim to where you are."

"Don't do that," said Max. "I think Gaffer and I can manage this. We're going to get out of the boat now. I'll call you in a few minutes if there's anything I need." Max hung up the handset and tilted the lower units until they were out of the water. He then joined Gaffer in the calf-deep water.

Max and Gaffer each took a line tied from the bow and led *Bimini Twist* away from the spoil area. Gaffer was of good cheer about the incident, happy that it did not result in damage to the hull. He teased his father a few times, but nothing serious and nothing nasty. Max laughed at himself and it helped release the tension of the dangerous cruising they had been doing. It was nerve racking to run at night in shallow water that the charts had told him to stay away from.

It was not the two hundred feet Max thought it was. It was more like one hundred. When the water came above Max's knees he decided they could ride the rest of the way. First Gaffer climbed the ladder and Max followed. Gaffer wound up the dock lines while Max lowered the motors and started them up. It sounded good to hear the healthy roar, and it felt good to be in water deep enough to navigate. Five minutes later they were idling up to the rickety marina dock picking up Cecil, Chet and their four companions.

187

"*Lady Liberty*, we're all aboard. What are your instructions?" Max waited.

Cameron called back, "How long will it take you to get to Spirit Cay?"

"Hold on," said Max. "Let me look at the chart."

While Max referred to the chart, Cecil spoke to Cameron. "What's up?"

"I think they've gone to Spirit Cay to drop off the girl. We followed them on radar to what looks like that location."

"What do you want us to do?" asked Cecil.

"If you can get in there, I want you to see if you can effect a rescue. So far they still don't know that we're involved. We still have the upper hand on them."

Max had finished his examination of the chart. He picked up the mike. "Cameron, if those guys went to Spirit Cay, they must really know their way around this area. I can try to get there, it's only about eight miles up the way but it's surrounded by smaller islands and very shallow water. I'll try it if you say so, but you might have to come rescue me."

Cameron had been looking at the same chart as Max. He could see the problem. He called back, "How would you feel about going back around the south end of Normans Cay and approach Spirit Cay from Exuma Sound. It'll take you another half hour to get back around Normans and then you'll have good water around you all the way to Spirit. Cecil and his men can land on the eastern shore and hoof it across the island. It won't take them more than ten or fifteen minutes to make it all the way across."

Max looked at Cecil. "What do you think?" Then into the handset he said, "Hold a minute." Cecil looked at the chart. He saw all the spoil banks and shallow areas on the western side of the island. He shook his head. His finger traced the route back past Normans, through Norman's Cut and out into the Exuma Sound. The water all looked good and the trek across the island when they got to Spirit Cay did not bother him.

Cecil picked up the mike. "We're going to do it your way, approach Spirit from the east. I want to get moving and we can't get anywhere approaching from the west. What's the latest on their boat."

Cameron responded. "From the radar scan it looks very much like their boat is now at the island. No matter what, somebody is going to have to go there and pick up the girl. Just be prepared to run into the kidnappers while you're at it."

"All right, we're on our way," responded Max.. "Call if you see anything on the radar or if you hear from them."

"OK," said Cameron. "I'll be in touch."

Cecil turned to Max. "How fast can this thing go?" he asked.

"I'll tell you what, with all this idling and near grounding, it's dying to shake out the cobwebs. What's that distance?" asked Max, tracing a route south across the bank, then east through Normans Cut and then north through Exuma Sound.

"Looks like fifteen miles, maybe twenty at most."

"Thirty minutes at most if we don't run aground," said Max.

"Then there's your answer," said Cecil. "Don't run aground."

NINETEEN

Spirit Cay

Axle Wolfe was angry with Tiny and had remained that way all day. When they arrived at Spirit Cay, he continued with the terse orders and insults. They beached their boat and walked up the sandy embankment to search out a place for Katie to await her rescuers. Axle added another of his barbary insults to the dozen or so he had already leashed upon Tiny. The big man's temper flared. He had been hearing it all day and finally he had heard enough. He grabbed Axle by the collar and lifted him off his feet. Axle wriggled and kicked and finally connected with the big man's knee. That was all Tiny was going to take from this little pipsqueak. He drew back and threw a jackhammer of a punch at Axle's gut. The loud mouthed runt doubled over in excruciating pain. He held his middle and writhed on the ground. It took him nearly a minute before he could force air back into his system and as soon as he did, dizzying nausea overcame him. When he was able to come somewhat under control, he crawled away from Tiny, mumbled something indistinguishable, and promised himself to keep a distance.

But Tiny had something to say. He had all of this caper he wanted, and his only wish was to see that the girl was returned safely to her parents. He stood over the cowering Axle. Stingray stood nearby in silence.

"I don't care what you do," said Tiny. "You go get your ransom money or whatever. I'm not going with you. I'm staying with the girl. You go send her parents here to pick her up. I'll risk capture, but I won't leave her here by herself. She'd be scared to death. Now, you go get your blood money and get out of my sight."

Axle and Stingray huddled for a few minutes, speaking in quiet, conspiratorial tones. The bottom line was that Tiny was now a liability to the venture, and the $500,000 split two ways, instead of three ways, had a great deal of appeal. Axle considered giving Tiny a final shove before they parted company, but the aching in his gut reminded him of just how bad an idea that was.

While Axle and Stingray made final preparations to collect the money, *Bimini Twist* cleared Normans Cut and headed north in the Exuma Sound. It would be offshore of Spirit Cay in fifteen minutes. Max switched off his running lights but kept the throttle opened wide. They were now in safe water with no fear of touching bottom. It was a relaxing feeling to have good water under the hull and no threat of running aground or a terrible collision. Max let the wind blow through his face and hair. It was wonderful. He felt twenty pounds lighter.

The radio on board *Lady Liberty* came alive. "Are you on station where I told you to be?" asked Axle.

"Exactly where you said," replied Jordan Deere. "I'm ready now. How is my daughter?"

"Your daughter is fine. I'm coming for the ransom soon. Stay right there." Axle clicked off. He and Stingray put their shoulders to the boat and shoved it away from the beach. When the water was waist deep the men scrambled on board and Stingray started the engine. He backed around, turned hard left in reverse and, when he was parallel to the shore, placed the gear control into forward, turned the wheel hard right, and headed seaward.

As soon as the kidnappers were fifty yards offshore Cameron picked up the small boat on the radar. He now knew for certain that the girl was being held on Spirit Cay, but he did not know how many men were holding her, or what weapons they might have. There was not much he could do but pay the kidnappers and hope for a safe release.

On Spirit Cay, Tiny and Katie found an area of short grass that had the look of a manicured lawn. He spread two towels together and lay back for a rest. Katie snuggled against the big man's shoulder and within two minutes was sleeping like a baby. Tiny closed his eyes and considered his situation. He was an accessory to the kidnaping, and for that he would have to face charges. On the other hand, he knew that if he surrendered peaceably and gave testimony against Axle and Stingray, he could mitigate his punishment. He shut his eyes and allowed himself to enjoy the closeness of Katie's childlike innocense. Being a comfort to her was its own reward.

The radio on *Bimini Twist* squawked. "Cecil, they're moving."

"From what location?" asked Cecil.

"From the midpoint of Spirit Cay on its western side. I can see the boat coming at us at about twenty knots. It will be here in about a half hour."

"That doesn't give us much time to find the girl," said Cecil.

"Do your best," said Cameron. "If we have to, we'll give up the money and try to go back and recover it later. Our main objective right now is to get the girl back safely."

"OK," said Cecil. "We're two miles off Spirit Cay right now. We can be ashore in about five minutes. I'll keep you posted."

"All right, I'll wait for your call." Cameron clicked off and hung up the microphone. "Cecil, can I ask you something?" asked Gaffer.

"Sure, what?"

"Are you a captain?"

"I'm a captain in the Defense Force. Not a sea captain."

"That's what I mean, captain in the Defense Force."

"Yep, I am."

"Isn't Cameron a sergeant?"

"He's a lieutenant."

Gaffer looked confused. "I thought he was a sergeant."

Cecil explained. "Cameron was a sergeant when you first met him. He's been in the Defense Force a long time and they finally made him a lieutenant."

"So you're a captain and he's a lieutenant. Who has the higher rank?"

"Oh, I see what you're getting at. A captain outranks a lieutenant but Cameron ran this operation and I took orders from him."

"Yeah," said Gaffer. "I was wondering about that."

"Let's see how I can explain this." Max leaned forward and looked at Cecil. He was wondering the same thing. "We both do different things. You saw it on this operation. I'm a special ops officer. I know how to move across the ground, and the water, to root out the bad guys. Cameron has been in the Defense Force ten years longer than me. He chose to be an enlisted man until they practically forced him to wear those silver bars, but he's probably the best strategist we have. He tells me what he wants done and I use what I've learned to go do it. He can't do what I do, and I can't do what he does. So the rank is not something we allow ourselves to stumble over. We just do our jobs."

In a low, admiring tone Max responded, "You sure do."

Max let the men off in three teams of two. Cecil and one officer started their sweep from the south end of the island and headed north. Chet took a man and headed west from the north/south midpoint of the island, and then Max ferried the last two men to the northern end of the island and let them off. The men would sweep west toward the point from which Cameron had told them that the kidnappers had departed a few minutes earlier.

A check of the chart told Gaffer that this water was every bit as bad as the water around Normans Cay. It was surrounded by reefs and rocks at both its northern and southern ends. There was nothing but shallow water all around. In most areas there was no more than three feet of water at low tide. It was now dead low. Gaffer just shook his head in disgust. "When are we going to get a break?"

Max shared his foul outlook. "Not tonight, I'm afraid." He too shook his head. "It's back to the old routine. Take your position."

Gaffer grabbed his biggest spotlight and placed a cushion on the bow. He took a seat and shined the light into the water ahead. He raised his hand in a signal to have his father move forward. They had a mile of bad water to negotiate. At no more than idle speed it would take thirty minutes to reach the beach on the western shore of the island. The tension left Max's neck and shoulders wracked with pain as the boat moved slowly forward and he looked over the side the whole time, seeing large dark spots go by underneath, frowning the whole time. It was a slow go.

Axle and Stingray moved inexorably toward *Lady Liberty*. The yacht was aglow with all of its helm lights, overhead lights, spot lights, and its anchor light. Ten minutes after they left the island, the two men could begin to see it on the horizon. Axle drove the boat as Stingray sat in silence. This was the testy part of the caper. Would the parents remain cooperative and toss the money to them, or would they have guns ready to take the kidnappers into custody? Both men hoped for the former result. Axle called to Jordan Deere. "We're gonna be there in a few minutes. Come to the back of the boat and bring the money."

Jordan replied. "I'll be waiting. The money is ready. When will you release my daughter."

"When we get the money and are clear of your boat, the people holding your daughter will call you and tell you where to find her." Axle clicked off.

From the research that Cameron was doing, Jordan was certain that Katie was being held on Spirit Cay only a dozen miles away, but there was nothing he could do about it. He had no idea who or how many people were holding her on the island, so he would go along with whatever he was told to do. His daughter's safety was the only issue here. The money, catching the bad guys, all other considerations took a back seat. Jordan was within a few miles and less than an hour from the most important person in his life, he would take no chances now.

Cameron told Jeremy Diamond to make the yacht ready to go. To the extent possible he wanted the option to move quickly. If the kidnappers boat was still on the radar screen when Cecil recovered Katie, Cameron would chase them down. He did not intend for this crime to go unpunished.

The lights on *Lady Liberty* were getting closer. In the dark night Axle's depth perception was shot. He could not tell if he was one mile or two from he yacht. He took his ancient twenty-five caliber Baretta from a worn out, filthy duffel bag and stuck it in his belt. He did not want to wave it in front of the people on *Lady Liberty*, but he did want them to see it as an expression of his seriousness and as an intimidation measure.

He brought his boat to within about one hundred yards of the yacht. It looked like a party on board. He could see at least five people on deck. Axle keyed his mike. "Mr. Deere, I am about to approach your stern. Come to that location and hold the money aloft. Those other people I see, I want them to go below. You are to be the only person on deck when we make the transfer. Do you understand?"

Jordan called back that the instruction was clear. Disappointed, Cameron sent the Diamonds and Abbey Deere below. He took out his forty-five and placed it on the bench seat. "Do you know how to use this?" he asked.

"Some," replied Jordan.

"It's loaded, there's a round chambered, and it's cocked. If you need it, just point and start shooting. It's automatic and loaded with twelve rounds. If lead starts flying this way and you need to protect yourself, don't stop shooting until it's empty. And then get your head down as fast as possible. Me and my men will be climbing over you to establish fire superiority. You don't want to get in the way."

Cameron backed down into the companionway. He could not be seen from behind the transom, but from this location he could be on the deck in two seconds. His men lined up behind him with weapons drawn, ready to move.

TWENTY

Problems Solved

After thirty minutes of creeping across the island, Cecil came to the top of a low hillock. He crawled to its top and lay prone on the ground. With his starlight binoculars he was able to see the entire half mile distance to the beach on the western coast of Spirit Cay. He scanned the area to his right, and at about a half mile to the north he could see Chet **and** his partner creeping slowly up the same bluff. He backed down the **rise** just enough so that he would be hidden from view of anyone watching from the west. He keyed his mouthpiece.

"Chet, come in."

"Here."

"I see you at about a half mile. Can you see me?"

"Hold one," said Chet. He scanned the area to his left. Cecil's partner waved. "I've got you."

"Hold your position. I'm going to give the area to the west a good look. I'll be right back with you."

"Ten-four."

Cecil crawled on his belly back over the top of the rise. Through a grey green haze he looked for images that looked out of place. He could see nothing out of the ordinary. "Chet, I don't see anything. This is what Cameron thought was the most likely location for the hostage."

"We still don't know everything about this site. It's too dark **to see** well. I say we should proceed with caution down to the beach."

"I agree. Take the territory slowly, fifty yards at a time. Go slow, quietly and keep your eyes open."

"You got it," replied Chet. He relayed to the team to his north. "Blue team, did you hear that?"

"Absolutely," came the response. "To let you know," he continued, "I have a visual on you at about a quarter mile to my south. I'm nearly at the beach. It's rocky, and it looks like a dropoff to the water. I'm being forced to converge to the south and west. I should meet up with you soon."

"That's good," said Chet. "Keep doing what you're doing. But don't get to the beach before me."

"Ten-four."

Before Cecil left his location at the crest of the hill, he looked out to sea. He could see *Bimini Twist* converging on the beach from the water side. The boat was either moving very slowly or stopped. Max and Gaffer had either run aground, or their progress was as slow as his own.

The three teams moved slowly and carefully toward the beach, a few feet at a time. No hurry, nice and easy. Kidnappers were somewhere near, and they had a hostage who was a young girl, probably sacred to death. Easy does it.

Axle pulled to within one hundred yards of *Lady Liberty*. It looked as if Jordan was alone on the deck, but he could not be certain. He called over, "Deere, who's that on the deck with you?"

Jordan Deere was confused, "What do you mean? There's **only** me. My wife is below and I'm alone at the helm where the radio is. I'm alone!"

"Good thing," replied Axle. "That's the way I want it. I'm moving toward you. Come to the back of the boat and have the money with you."

Jordan took the duffel to the stern. His heart raced as he waited for the kidnappers to approach. He turned around and could see Cameron half in and half out of the cabin. It gave him a small measure of comfort to know that he was covered.

Axle placed the gear shift lever into forward and idled slowly toward the yacht. His heart also raced as he shortened the distance between himself and the half million dollar ransom.

Cecil was now 250 yards closer to the beach. He dropped to the ground and called to Chet. "Anything?"

"Nothing yet," came the response.

From his spot only thirty yards away Tiny heard Cecil's call. Katie was sound asleep using the big man's chest as a pillow. He knew it was up for him. He did not want to startle the girl so he gently nudged her. She did not respond. He nudged her again and she stirred. He whispered, "Katie, wake up."

Her eyes opened. "Katie, your rescuers are here, wake up."

Katie raised her head and shook off the sleep. "They're here?" she asked.

"Yes, they're here. It's time for you to go."

Katie squeezed Tiny and held him tightly for a few seconds. Tiny broke the embrace. "Are you ready?" he asked. Katie nodded vigorously. "OK, keep your head down and I'll call them."

"I'm ready," whispered Katie.

"OK," said Tiny. "Here we go." He sat up where he might be seen.

"Hello!" he bellowed.

Cecil heard the greeting and plastered himself into the ground. He called to Chet. "I have contact!"

"Hello," called Tiny. "I have the girl. I want to turn her over to you. I'm not armed and I mean to give no resistance."

Cecil heard the call and tuned in to the direction of the voice. He looked over and could see the big man sitting up, holding still, and making no moves at all in an attitude of submission. The girl was standing next to Tiny. She looked OK, not scared or hysterical.

Cecil called over. "I'm Captain Cecil Hunter of the Royal Bahamas Defense Force. Your position is surrounded. Send the girl to me." He and his partner stood and shone their flash lights onto the ground in front of their position.

"Go ahead," Tiny said to Katie. "It'll be all right."

Katie hugged Tiny's neck. She began to cry. "What will happen to you?"

"Don't worry about me," said Tiny. "You go with those men and they'll take you to your mom and dad."

"I love you, Tiny," she said.

Tiny hugged the girl for the last time. "I know, Sweetie. Now you go be where you can be safe. I have to let these men take me." Katie gave one more squeeze and then ran to where Cecil was shining his light. Cecil dropped to one knee and received the girl.

"Are you all right?" he asked.

"Yes," she replied.

"My name is Cecil, and I'm here to take you to your parents. You're safe now."

"Sir," said the girl, "I was always safe. Tiny took care of **me** the whole time. He never let me be afraid; he protected me from **the** other men. He always made sure I was never hurt or afraid. Please let him go."

Tiny stood in the background with his hands raised high in the air. Cecil could see that he posed no threat and wanted to be taken in peacefully. He turned to his companion. "Go ahead and cuff him. No rough stuff." He accompanied his man to where Tiny stood. Tiny placed his hands behind his back to receive the cuffs.

Katie went to where the giant stood and hugged his leg. "I love you, Tiny. Don't let them take you."

"It's OK Sweetie. I'll be OK, and you're safe. That's all that matters."

As soon as the big man was in cuffs, Cecil activated his radio. "We have the girl. She's safe and unharmed, and the situation is secure."

Jordan Deere stood poised at the back of the boat with the duffel in his hand. Axle was now only ten feet away and carefully closing the distance. As he came broadside to *Lady Liberty's* transom he reversed his engine to glide to a stop. "Throw down the money," he called.

Jordan could see the pistol sticking out of Axle's belt. It was ugly and threatening. As Jordan held the duffel for Axle to grab, the radio call came. Jordan heard the call, but he was certain Axle could not from his position below the transom, and with the sound of his outboard drowning out the sound. Jordan turned with the duffel in his hand. His expression was asking Cameron what to do next. He yanked the duffel back but Axle had a grip on it and tugged against him with one hand, while grabbing for his gun with the other. Jordan fell back to avoid any stray bullets. Axle took just a second to toss the duffel over to Stingray, and hit the throttle to the full open position. The boat began to move away and was fifteen feet from *Lady Liberty* when Cameron bolted out of the cabin door followed by his Defense Force officers. He snatched up his forty-five as he passed the bench seat and was at the transom in no time. He let go a burst of fire at the boat, aiming at the engine and trying not to connect with either of the men. An instant later two of his men were also tossing lead while another shot off a series of illumination flairs that lit up the sky all around.

Cameron and his men could now see perfectly. A ruptured **fuel** line had slowed the small boat to a ten knot crawl. At a fifty yard distance it sat in the circle of light, helpless, trying to move slowly away. Cameron authorized his men to take target practice at the boat's outboard, but to not shoot at its passengers unless they shot back.

Axle and Stingray knew immediately that it was over for them. They stood with their hands high in the air. Axle held his pistol high aloft and made a dramatic display of tossing it in the ocean. He wanted the police to know for certain that he no longer posed a threat.

One of Cameron's men had an unusual request. "Sir, the men have been cooped up all day on this boat. They have pent up energy and need a release. Could we take some target practice?"

"I told you I don't want you to hurt those men."

"No, Sir. That's not what I mean. We'd just like to put a few holes in that hull."

Cameron considered this for a minute and a wide grin crossed his face. "Go ahead, sink it. But don't hit the prisoners."

Six Defense Force officers stood at the transom of *Lady Liberty* and fired single shots into the small boat. They aimed at a point just below the waterline and their bullets, one after another, created leaks in its hull. Water poured in from dozens of bullet holes as the boat began leaking like a sieve. Soon the water was up to the seats. Axle and Stingray understood what was happening. A hundred bullets were tossed in their direction and none had hit them. They knew that no one was going to shoot them, but it was no fun being on the receiving end or a barrage. They donned life jackets and tied a buoy to the ransom-filled duffel as they knew that soon enough they would be floating free of the sinking vessel.

TWENTY-ONE

Together Again at Last

The three teams met up at the spot where Cecil and his partner had discovered Katie and Tiny. Because Tiny was subdued and appeared to pose no threat, the reunion was relaxed. Katie had received kind words from each of the men and she knew for certain that her ordeal was over. It would now only be a matter of time before she would be with her parents. A signal came across Cecil's earpiece.

"Cecil, how's your situation?"

"The teams have all rendezvoused at my location. All my men are accounted for. No injuries, a successful mission. How's your situation?"

"More good news," said Cameron. "We have the kidnappers in custody. We have the money. We also had their boat but it sprung a leak or two and sank. It's all good."

Cecil did not fully understand the import of the part about the boat springing a leak or two, but he was happy to hear that the operation had been successful. A moment later Cecil's radio came alive again. It was Gaffer.

"Well, guys, it's not all good here."

"What's the matter, Gaff?" asked Cecil.

"We made it to about a half mile from your location, but it's way low tide and the water was just too shallow to go under power. Right now we have the engines tilted full up and my father is walking in the water up to only his knees, pulling the boat by a dock line. I'm about to join him."

"I'm sending help right now," said Cecil. He motioned for two of his men to go intercept the boat and help out.

"No, no," said Gaffer. "That's not necessary. It's not something that's difficult to do, it's just a nuisance. We're just hoping that the water doesn't get any shallower."

"Do you want me to send my men or not?" asked Cecil.

"No," replied Gaffer. "We'll be to your location in less than a half hour." Then Gaffer hung up the mike and jumped into the water with his father. He held the flashlight on the water ahead of where Max was walking to help maneuver around any protruding rocks.

Cecil led the group to the water's edge to await pickup by *Bimini Twist*. After such an intense night, he hoped there would be no problem with it being able to get his team, and Tiny and Katie, away from Spirit Cay. He keyed his radio, "Cameron, did you hear Gaffer?"

"I heard," replied Cameron. "How do you want to handle it?"

"For one thing, don't come in too close to this island. The water around here is really not navigable in a big boat, barely in a small boat. You can come inshore a few miles if you want. We'll do what we can to get *Bimini Twist* up and running and then rendezvous with you ASAP."

"OK," said Cameron. "We're going to come in about eight miles. We'll be four miles offshore which is about all we dare to."

"We'll find you there," came the reply.

Cecil did not like leaving Max and Gaffer out there to walk the boat in by themselves. They had had the roughest night of anyone, and now they were walking their boat across the rocks and sandbars. In spite of Gaffer's protest, he sent a team of men to go give them a hand.

Katie sat with Tiny on the bank just above the sandy beach. Her arm was through his and her head was resting against him. Cecil took this in, as did Chet. To a little girl who was helpless and afraid, the big man had been a savior. They would remember this relationship and make certain it was noted for the record when charges were brought against the kidnappers. They wondered how such a gentle man could become involved in a plot like this. It seemed so out of character.

Forty minutes passed before *Bimini Twist* could be seen, now only a hundred yards off. Cecil used his night vision binoculars to see what was happening. He could see Max and Gaffer sitting at the helm. It appeared that they were referring to a navigational chart spread out on the leaning post. Two of his men, in water little more than ankle deep, were towing *Bimini Twist* by ropes tied off the bow, while a third was walking ahead of them shining a flashlight into the water. It would not be long now.

On board *Lady Liberty* the prisoners' hands were cuffed and their legs were shackled. They were tied together and tethered to the fighting chair in the cockpit. They weren't going anywhere. Jeremy Diamond was at the helm, navigating on a course of 110 degrees at a speed of twelve knots. His GPS told him that he would be four miles off Spirit Cay in forty-five minutes. Jessica Diamond sat on the bench seat holding Abbey Deere's hand to calm her. The anticipation of the moment had passed and she was having a physical letdown. Days without sleep and worrying for her daughter's safety had caught up with her. She was emotionally drained and shook from fatigue.

"Abbey, you're going to be with your little girl in a short while, probably less than an hour. She's OK, so you need to pull yourself together and show a strong front. She has been traumatized and she's probably exhausted. She'll need you to be strong.."

"I know," said Abbey. "You're right. I'm going to freshen up and make myself ready to see her." She stood, but before she headed down the stairs to the cabin she took the seat next to Jeremy Diamond. She put an arm around his neck and squeezed him. "I don't know how I'll ever be able to thank you two. You're the best friends a person could ever hope to know. I love you both so much."

Jeremy accepted her affection and returned the platonic embrace. "Knowing Katie is safe is all the thanks I could ever ask for. Getting her back is its own reward. Now go make yourself presentable to your daughter. She'll be here soon." Then to his wife he asked, "Honey, when's the last time you had something to eat? Now that the tension is behind us I find that I'm starved."

Abbey, half way through the cabin door, turned around. "That's an excellent idea. We can kill time by feeding our men. What about all these policemen too?"

Jessica's face lit up. "Let's do it. We can keep busy in the galley until Katie arrives. I'll bet the men on shore could use a meal too. Max Carson just filled the refrigerator this morning. Let's get busy."

Abbey Deere took five minutes to wash her face and apply some new powder and lipstick. Her hair, which had been neglected for nearly three days, she combed into a bun and pinned it up. She was now ready to attack the kitchen and ultimately see her daughter. Jordan Deere stayed at the helm with Jeremy and Cameron as the miles slowly passed under *Lady Liberty's* keel.

Bimini Twist finally made it to the beach. Cecil's men were covered with salt and sand and were anxious to climb aboard and get off this island. Gaffer knew that *Bimini Twist* had been through an ordeal, but he could not remember anyone tracking dirt or sand on the boat. For this reason he believed there was still hope that no permanent scratches had been put in the boat's finish. He stood at the dive ladder with the fresh water hose and washed down the shoes of each person as he entered. It made sense to try to keep the boat from being damaged. They had been in some tight spots this day and they had taken great risks in very dangerous waters. But, they had not touched bottom once with the hull or the props. There was still a good possibility of coming out of this with no damage. Gaffer thought about all the dirt and grime he saw on the boat's deck when he first saw it in Bimini the previous evening. He cringed thinking about what a mess it had been. He vowed to never let that happen again. The hull might be four years old, but it still looked new and he wanted to keep it that way.

When the last man was aboard and Katie had climbed up onto the jump seat next to Tiny, Max hit the starters and backed away from the shore. He spun the boat around and headed seaward. Cecil sat on the leaning post next to Max while Gaffer took his seat on the bow looking into the water for obstructions. In five minutes the depth finder registered ten feet of water under the transducer. Max called to his son, "Gaffer, it's deep enough. You can come back here now."

Gaffer slowly climbed down from the bow. He was not moving well, his joints were stiff and his muscles were sore. He made his way back to the helm to join his father and Cecil. They too looked tired and achy. It seemed like everyone could use some rest and relaxation.

Soon a light glowed on the horizon. In the darkness Max could not tell if the distance was two miles or three. But he was the father of two sons himself, and he knew that the reunion of Katie with her parents had to take place with the utmost of haste. The entire purpose for being there was only minutes away. He leaned on the throttle and sped up to thirty-eight knots.

Jordan and Abbey Deere could see the running lights on *Bimini Twist* in the distance. They stood at the transom, Jordan with his arm around his wife's shoulder hardly able to contain their excitement. At first a small light on the horizon, and then brighter, and then close enough to make out the red and the green nav lights on the bow. The boat was coming at them at an amazing speed, rushing their one and only Katie to the reunion. At fifty yards off *Lady Liberty's* stern, Max throttled back and *Bimini Twist* came off its plane. He still maintained ten knots just to clear the distance between the two boats a little faster.

Jordan moved to the swim platform. As *Bimini Twist* approached, he held it off so there would be no bumping against the yacht. Next Cecil handed Katie across to him. She wrapped her arms and legs around her father and gave him a boa constrictor squeeze. They buried their heads in each other's shoulders and held on tight. Abbey walked out onto the swim platform and Katie turned her attention to her. There was a family hug that lasted and lasted.

Cecil tossed a line over to Cameron who tied it to a cleat. Max shut down the engines. The silence was wonderful. Jordan moved his family into the cockpit. There were hugs for the Diamonds as well. Jordan introduced his daughter to Cameron and pointed out the other Defense Force officers who helped to catch the kidnappers. Katie shrank back when she saw Axle in shackles sitting on the deck tied to the fighting chair. She was tempted to kick him as she walked by, but made a better choice and just kept going. Jordan led his family down the stairs to the cabin.

It took a good twenty minutes for everyone to settle down and let the realization sink in that little Katie Deere was now safe with her parents. Her mother continuously stroked Katie's hair until Katie had to take her hand away and hold it to keep it still.

On deck there were too many people and too much milling around. Cameron decided to put all the prisoners, along with six of his guards on *Bimini Twist*. That left a more reasonable number of people on *Lady Liberty*. Before anyone left to board *Bimini Twist*, Cecil made it known that Tiny had cooperated and was to be treated gently. He was a special prisoner who would receive special handling.

It took a while but eventually it was discovered that Jessica and Abbey had made a mountain of food for anyone who wanted it. They had fourteen Defense Force operatives to feed, the Diamonds, Carsons, Deeres, and three prisoners. Soon the mountain had turned into a collection of empty platters, so Jeremy and Jessica Diamond got busy in the galley for a second round of food preparation. Gaffer walked around the boat with a jug of water in one hand and a liter of Ginger Ale in the other. He made it clear to Jeremy that for this occasion only he would help with the service. But he wanted him to remember that first and foremost he was a fishing mate. Jeremy promised that this would be the only time he would ever ask him to pour drinks on board *Lady Liberty*. They had a laugh over it, but Gaffer had made his point.

As the celebration continued, Jeremy, Cameron and Max made plans. Everyone on board was exhausted from sleep deprivation, anxiety, a day filled with tension and relief. Jeremy had called back to rent several rooms at the tiny motel on Highborne Cay. They did not have to stay at anchor to enjoy the moment. They could head in while the party went on. Gaffer took what was now his seat at the helm and hit the starters on the big diesels. They roared to life. He made certain he had all his navigation lights on and noticed that the radar was ready to go. He hit the switch for the winch and heard the powerful motor lift the anchor from the sea bottom.

Max joined him at the helm for a look at the electronic chart. A heading of due north for one mile and then an angle to about sixty degrees would place them on a course to pick up the channel markers leading into the dockage at Highborne. Gaffer looked around to make certain there were no obstructions in their way. Max had an idea that would keep them out of trouble.

"I'll lead the way in the *Twist*. I'll keep my eye on the bottom and you follow me fifty to a hundred yards behind. That way I'll see any shallow water long before it becomes a hazard to you."

They agreed on this and Max moved over to his own boat. Cecil untied them and Max backed away from *Lady Liberty*. He executed a 180 and idled toward Highborne. Gaffer turned in a wide arc and lined up in his father's wake.

On this dark night, when so much had happened, and so many lives had been touched by men, some so mean, and others so brave, Max Carson, on board *Bimini Twist,* moved at idle speed to the safety of port. He looked back to see *Lady Liberty* turn to line up in his wake. He swelled with pride as he watched his son sitting at the helm of the great fishing yacht. His boy was becoming a man, taking a role as a leader among other adults and gaining the respect of yachtsmen, fishermen, and the officers of the Royal Bahamas Defense Force.

Epilogue

A small crowd had gathered in the dockage area awaiting the arrival of the boats carrying the kidnap victim. When they arrived, a spontaneous party erupted. Naturally everyone was celebrating the successful return of the little girl. It was happy faces all around except for those of the three prisoners who were made to sit on the tarmac and lean against the skids of the helicopters while everyone else enjoyed themselves. Katie brought her parents and the Diamonds over to meet Tiny, and explained to them that he was the one who kept her safe and kept her from being scared. They thanked him for that consideration and promised to be at his trial to say a few kind words.

But the hour was getting late and all the energy had run out for the day. Soon the party dispersed, there was profuse thanks from the Deeres and the Diamonds to the members of the Defense Force, and to the Carsons for all the sacrifices they had made to help the dangerous situation result in a successful, happy ending.

Within two hours of the time the boats docked in the marina, the three helicopters took off from Highborne Cay. The private one headed back to the mainland carrying Jeremy and Jessica Diamond, and Jordan, Abbey, and Katie Deere. The military copters took fourteen volunteers of the Defense Force and three prisoners to their headquarters in Nassau. The motel rooms that had been rented were given to Cameron Ford, Cecil Hunter, and Chet Cristy. Max and Gaffer spent the night on board *Lady*

213

Liberty, with *Bimini Twist* safely docked and floating in the next slip over.

Cameron, Cecil and Chet joined Max and Gaffer in the comfortable seats surrounding *Lady Liberty's* helm. They simply wanted to relax, sip on a beer or a soft drink, and let the adrenaline run off. Compared to the noise and activity of the day, running around in the boats, sneaking and peeping on the islands, and the gunfire to subdue the kidnappers, this relaxing moment was welcome.

"That was a beautiful fish you caught this morning," Gaffer told Cecil.

"I never knew it could be so much fun," he replied. "I've only fished a little in my life. I've caught a few small snappers, I think a grouper once. A couple of barracuda for certain. But that one this morning was the best."

"Yeah," said Gaffer, "a nice dolphin like that one could get you hooked."

"Is that a play on words?" asked Cameron. It had made him chuckle.

"Like hooked on fishing?" asked Gaffer.

Cameron chuckled again. "Something like that."

"But it could," said Gaffer. Max and Cecil nodded.

"It certainly could," said Cecil.

The conversation turned to the return trip to Bimini set for the following morning. *Bimini Twist* was to be towed back to Bimini behind *Lady Liberty*. They decided to have a leisurely morning, not rush to get on the water at the crack of dawn. There was no reason to be in a hurry. Gaffer turned on the chart plotter and examined the area. They would be crossing the Tongue of the Ocean on the way back. These waters were known to produce some amazing game fish that thrived on the **massive** quantities of bait fish that followed the currents in this area.

"It's a shame to be here and not put a line in the water," he said. "There's a lot of territory to cover between here and Bimini."

"So, we'll slow down and you can troll back," said Max.

"Towing the *Twist?*" asked Gaffer. That didn't make any sense.

Since that would not work, Max lost interest in the conversation and the subject was changed. But Gaffer was determined. He thought about the possibilities and soon a plan came to mind. He interrupted the conversation.

"I've got it," he said. "We won't tow the *Twist* back. Dad, you can drive it back to Bimini and I'll drive this one. That way we can both fish on the way back."

The idea became popular and soon it had developed into a two boat fishing tournament with the losing team having to wash both boats when they arrived in port. The difficult part was how to give Gaffer enough of a handicap to make the contest fair. When it was suggested that he would have to use *Bimini Twist* he did not object. He said that would give **him** an opportunity to 'run and gun'. That meant that he could run all over the place every time he saw what looked like a school, or birds or floating debris. He liked the idea of the mobility he would have in the smaller boat. He liked it so much in fact that the men took that advantage away from him and said he would have to skipper the yacht. That was OK too, because on *Lady Liberty* he had a tower from where he could see miles ahead and further down into the water.

Both ways of fishing had advantages, so it was decided that the only possible way of equalizing the contest was to give Gaffer the weakest fisherman to be on his team. Now everyone was protesting that they were the weakest, because everyone wanted to be on the boat Gaffer was on. Even Max tried to make an argument for why he should fish with Gaffer, but no one was buying it.

They looked again at the chart and saw that Bimini was nearly 150 miles from their present location and only forty miles of it were worth fishing. The plan changed again. They would not go to Bimini, they would go to Chub Cay in the Berry Islands. It was seventy miles, but the water was as good or better than the water in front of Bimini. Their chances of catching some serious fish were excellent.

So it was decided. Gaffer would fish off *Bimini Twist* with Chet and Cecil. Cameron would accompany Max on *Lady Liberty*. Cameron was grumbling that only luck would win them this one. Cecil and Chet were smiling.

Gaffer immediately walked over to *Bimini Twist* to see what kind of shape it was in for the tournament. He placed a half dozen rigged and a half dozen unrigged ballyhoo, along with two five pound blocks of squid into a bucket and returned it to the freezer on *Lady Liberty*. "There you go," he said. "Now we're even for bait. I'll get you a few artificials for trolling."

Max looked at the bait. "How about trading me these unrigged ballyhoo for your rigged ballyhoo?"

Gaffer looked at his father. He shrugged, "You'll have to rig your own. You can have all the rigging materials you need off the *Twist*."

Very disappointing news for Max. He was a terrible rigger, a real amateur. He asked Cameron if he knew how to rig the baits and received a disgusted groan. Finally he made a bargain with Gaffer. He would trade him all his unrigged baits for three rigged baits. Gaffer agreed. It was a much better deal for his team, he did not like anyone else's rigged baits anyway. He preferred to rig his own. Again Max looked defeated.

"We're screwed," he said to Cameron.

"Why?" asked Cameron.

Max gave a disappointed shake to his head. "Gaffer has fifteen baits, we have nine. His are going to be rigged by him, ours are out of the package. His will swim like distressed flying fish, ours will probably flop around until they fall apart."

"You're not making me feel any better," said Cameron. "What are our chances?"

Max just shook his head, "Not that good." He then heard the radio on *Bimini Twist* begin to broadcast the weather and tides. Max grumbled, "He's thought of everything," he said.

"What?" asked Cameron.

"He's getting the tides so he can put out his wahoo lures on the change. We can do the same thing but I was hoping he wouldn't think of that."

The men met in the cockpit of *Lady Liberty*. The rules were established. Since it was a seventy mile trek, they would have to average six knots to make it back in eleven hours. Rule one: They could not leave Highborne until 8:00 AM as *Bimini Twist* needed gas and the fuel dock did not open until 7:30. They had to touch down in Chub by 7:00 PM. Rule two: the most weight of dolphin, wahoo, and tuna won. Released billfish counted as fifty pounds each. Rule three: the losing boat not only cleaned both boats, but they also cleaned all the fish, and bought dinner for everyone. Those were the rules, nothing more.

Max and Gaffer agreed upon which equipment each boat would

carry. Since *Lady Liberty* now had no equipment, Max took an International Fifty, a Thirty and a Duel 6/0 from *Bimini Twist*. Gaffer had the same. Each boat had two light tackle spinning outfits and two TLD Twentys. Except for the spinning tackle, all the rods were Stars.

Gaffer emerged from the cabin the following morning groggy and sore. The adventures of the two previous days and nights had fatigued him so much that his sleep was deep and void of dreams. The sun was just above the horizon. A steady breeze from the northeast brought chilly winds and a quartering sea of two to four feet. Advantage *Lady Liberty*.

As Gaffer slid open the door to go outside, Cameron, Cecil and Chet walked up to the yacht with their duffels slung over their shoulders. It was none too early to get started. Max emerged from the shower and turned it over to Gaffer. When he was toweled off and dressed he started bringing the galley to life. Soon the smells of toast, coffee, and bacon filled the boat. The next three quarters of an hour were spent on a leisurely breakfast as everyone tried to shake off the sleep of the previous night.

Max turned on the weather radio to see what conditions would be like for today's run. He did not like what he heard for Gaffer's crossing, but it would be OK for his own. "You don't have to run *Bimini Twist* today if you don't want to. It's going to be pretty wet."

"What, two to four?" asked Gaffer.

"And chilly," added Max.

Gaffer was no fool when it came to the hazards of nautical navigation. He would not take unnecessary risks. "We'll see when we get out there," he said. "If it's bad I'll ride with you. Meanwhile, I still have work to do to get ready."

218

He left the cabin and drove *Bimini Twist* over to the fuel **dock**. It would be open in twenty minutes and he wanted to be the first one **served**. While he waited, he filled the fresh water tank and washed down the decks. By the time the dockmaster came around to unlock the pumps, the boat was clean and the baits were rigged. It was not quite eight o'clock when he cranked up the motors and idled back over to the slip next to *Lady Liberty*. He parked the boat, tied off and headed over to the yacht.

"Let's go, let's go," he called.

The door to the cabin slid open and the men emerged. Chet and Cecil helped Cameron and Max with dock lines and shore power, and then climbed aboard *Bimini Twist* with Gaffer. Breakfast had moved so slow that Gaffer was afraid the men had lost their enthusiasm for the two-boat tournament. But the opposite was true. Cecil was pumped and ready to go, and his enthusiasm had rubbed off on Chet.

Gaffer idled out of the marina and picked up the channel markers at the end of the small jetty. His depth finder was reading out six feet of water, so he pushed the throttles forward. A half mile later he was outside the shallows but still in the lee of the island. The wind was stiffer than he had previously thought. Small white caps flecked the surface of the sea and the boat pounded unmercifully at high speed. When he was four miles offshore and all the islands were dotted lines on the horizon, he slowed down and called his father.

"*Lady Liberty*, Dad, where are you."

The call came back, "Just idling out of the marina. Where are you?"

"I'm about five miles ahead of you just about to let lines out."

"OK, keep in touch if you need anything."

"I'll **let** you know." Next, with Cecil at the controls, Gaffer went to the stern and began sending lines overboard. With no outriggers, he chose a three line spread. Inside ten minutes they were trolling at six knots. Cecil and Chet were stoked for some action.

On *Lady Liberty* Cameron sat at the helm while Max prepared the baits. It took him twice as long to skirt his ballyhoos and create rough looking Haywire Twists. He used the yacht's high-tech outriggers and put out a five line spread with three ballyhoos and two artificials. For a measure of luck he tossed out a shiny foot long spoon with a 7/0 hook at the end. If there were fish in the area, he felt he had as good a chance as **Gaffer** to boat one. He and Cameron climbed up to the first platform of the **tower** where there were a set of controls. From there he could watch the lines as well as the surrounding area for any signs of life. He could also see *Bimini Twist* on the distant horizon.

It was as everyone expected. The area proved to have a **healthy** stock of fish. The dolphin were hitting regularly and by noon both boats had three in the box. The tuna proved elusive, but no one really thought that was much of a possibility as it was the opposite season for **them**. Perhaps the wahoo would show up.

Lady Liberty was now fishing no more than two miles off *Bimini Twist's* port beam. They talked to each other every half hour or so. From fifteen miles offshore, Nassau could be seen as they passed by.

At one thirty Max suggested to Gaffer that they pull their lines and that *Bimini Twist* accept a tow while everyone had lunch on board *Lady Liberty*. It was a popular idea, and within ten minutes all the lines were in and *Bimini Twist* was riding in the yacht's wide wake.

They took an hour's break from the fishing while they ate and visited. They told the stories of who caught which fish and how they were boated. Gaffer looked into *Lady Liberty's* fishbox and knew for **certain** that he was at least twenty pounds ahead in the contest. Both boats **were** even with only four remaining ballyhoos each. By the time lunch was over, they were only thirty miles from Chub Cay and into the final leg of the contest. Gaffer, along with his two anglers, climbed back over to *Bimini Twist* to continue the competition.

The radios were quieter than they had been during the morning. Each boat knew the other was catching fish because they could see it stop, or spin, or back down, and they could see the activity in the cockpit. But they were no longer calling each other quite so often so it was difficult to tell who was doing what. At three thirty, with Chub Cay on the horizon perhaps nine miles off, and just as the tide was changing from dead low, *Bimini Twist* hooked into a wahoo that was certain to finish off the competition. Gaffer knew his wahoo, and this one was seventy pounds if it was an ounce. Now the radio on *Lady Liberty* came to life.

"Dad, Dad. Come in."

Gaffer received no response so he kept calling. Finally a **hurried** Cameron came on the line. "Gaffer, we're busy." He dropped the microphone and continued doing what he was doing.

Gaffer looked over and could see that *Lady Liberty* was stopped but he could not distinguish what they were doing. His problem was that the fishbox was too small to hold the entire wahoo and he wanted permission to cut its head off. He decided to take the initiative and do it anyway. Certainly his father would not disqualify the fish on account of that.

Twenty minutes later his radio came to life. "Gaffer, what's up?"

"What's up with you?"

"We **were** busy. What do you need."

The excitement in his voice was evident. "We just won the tournament," said Gaffer. "This wahoo was at least sixty or seventy pounds. I was calling to ask if you'd mind if I cut it in half to fit it into the fishbox."

Max could not tell if Gaffer was serious or just trying to brag a little. "Go ahead and cut it. No Problem."

"Good, cause I already did. Dad, listen, we've been beat to death out here. What do you say we head in?"

"Yeah, let's head in. I have the charts on the screen. Follow **me** in, I'll knock the waves down for you."

"I'll be there in ten minutes." Each man took a rod and reeled it in. Gaffer secured the equipment in the rocket launcher and overhead rod holders. He tossed a couple of buckets of sea water over his decks **and** put away the rest of the bait and the bait knives. He throttled up and very soon was idling around *Lady Liberty*.

Max was just finishing up putting his gear away too. He used a wash down hose to clean the cockpit, hung it back up and then dried off on a towel. He returned to the helm and waved to Gaffer. He then placed the controls into forward gear and headed toward the channel for Chub Cay with *Bimini Twist* in his wake.

The Chub Cay Marina reluctantly answered the radio call, but when they finally answered they were happy to provide two slips for the boats. Gaffer went in first, docked *Bimini Twist* and then headed over to the other slip to help with *Lady Liberty's* dock lines. When the boat was secure and the shore power was hooked up, it was judging time. First Chet and Cecil hauled five nice sized dolphins, seeming to average twenty five to thirty-five pounds each, into the hand cart. Then each took a half of the **wa**hoo and placed that in the cart. They wheeled their catch over to the **scales** where a native boy was happy to weigh them for the men for fifty cents each. They accepted.

Total weight for the entire load, 204 pounds. A very good **day** by any standards, exceptional for *Bimini Twist*. Max and Cameron stoo**d by** to see what they were up against. This was much stiffer than they had imagined.

The wahoos they had caught were relatively small, **twenty**-six pounds and thirty-one. They also had four dolphins to weigh, but **they** did not look as big as the other men's. And as it turned out, they were not. They averaged twenty-eight pounds each. "It looks like our total weight coming across the dock will be only one sixty-nine," said Max.

Gaffer let out a hoot. He high fived his fishing companio**ns** and pranced around the dock hooting some more. Max was disappointed to see his son act so immaturely. "Sure, Gaffer, when you win a tournament you celebrate, but you do it like a gentleman."

"Sour grapes, sour grapes," said Gaffer. "You're just bu**mm**ed because you lost."

"I what?" asked Max. "Because I lost?"

"Yeah, because you lost," said Gaffer with a wide grin on his face. "You lost, one sixty-nine to two o four." Then he picked up a nearby hose and handed it to his father. "Start cleaning, Dad. I'll be in the club having a coke with Cecil and Chet." The two defense Force officers were grinning too, but not quite as foolishly as Gaffer.

"Oh," said Max. "I see, you think you won."

Gaffer quieted a little. "Yeah, two o four to one sixty-nine."

Max shook his head and pitied his son. Gaffer looked confused. "Two o four to one sixty-nine," he repeated, this time very subdued. Max looked at his son. Now Gaffer's smile was gone.

"A release?" asked Gaffer. Max pointed up to the top of his starboard outrigger. There, hanging from a clip was a red Offshore **Angler** tee shirt flapping in the breeze. Gaffer did not have to look too closely to see what it meant. The fish added fifty pounds to *Lady Liberty's* tally giving them a total of 219 pounds, fifteen more than *Bimini Twist's* total.

"You know, the boat is new. I couldn't find a striped **marlin flag** anywhere, so I used the tee shirt that has a picture of a blue on it. **I hope** that's OK."

Gaffer's mouth fell open. He looked again at the tee shirt hanging from the outrigger. He partially closed his mouth and croaked. "A **striped** marlin?"

Nonchalantly Max nodded his head. "Yeah, striped. About a hundred and twenty pounds. Good fight, beautiful fish, very healthy when we released him."

Max held out his hand and allowed Cecil and Chet, and **finally** Gaffer to shake it. "Yeah, a hundred and twenty pound striped marlin. A real beauty." He headed down the dock toward the club house. He called to his fishing companion, "Come on, Cameron. I'll buy you a beer. These guys are going to busy for a couple of hours and I need to get off my feet."

Max and Cameron walked down the dock knowing that the others were watching them. Without looking back both men gave a little wave. Winning was always good. Coming in second place, well, second place never feels quite as good as first place.

Printed in the United States
1109000001B